SEVENTEEN SERIES

SHORT STORY COLLECTION

A.D. STARRLING

COPYRIGHT

The Seventeen Series Ultimate Short Story Collection: #1-6

First Death (A Seventeen Series Short Story) #1
Copyright © AD Starrling 2014.
Dancing Blades (A Seventeen Series Short Story) #2
Copyright © AD Starrling 2015.
The Meeting (A Seventeen Series Short Story) #3
Copyright © AD Starrling 2015.
The Warrior Monk
(A Seventeen Series Short Story) #4
Copyright © AD Starrling 2015.
The Hunger (A Seventeen Series Short Story) #5
Copyright © AD Starrling 2015.
The Bank Job (A Seventeen Series Short Story) #6
Copyright © AD Starrling 2015.

www.ADStarrling.com
shop.adstarrling.com

Edited by Right Ink On The Wall

FIRST DEATH

A SEVENTEEN SERIES SHORT STORY

A.D. STARRLING

1570. Carpathian Mountains, Moldavia.

The shadows of the hunters danced between the trees, their forms at times insubstantial amongst the white flakes falling silently from the overcast night sky.

The boy knew all too well the deadly nature of the shapes chasing him through the forest. Blood pounded in his skull as he ran, the desperate thrum matching the cadence of his feet striking the snow covered ground. His breaths sounded unnaturally loud in his ears and masked the sounds of his pursuers. The sweat soaking his back had turned to icy trails, and frost crusted his eyes and nose. He ignored the stitch in his side, wiped at his face, and squinted at the dark landscape unfolding before him.

There was movement out the corner of his eye.

His heart stuttered in his chest as he spotted a gray shape. He looked around and counted four more monstrous forms closing in on him.

The spear carved the air with a silken sound. The boy watched breathlessly as it sliced through the water and impaled a fat trout. A sliver of blood flowed down the shaft of the weapon when the man lifted it from the river. The fish twisted and arched around the blade, its body glistening in the sunlight as it sought to escape. Its desperate twitches slowly stilled.

The man turned and smiled. 'Your turn, son.'

The boy gripped his own spear with white-knuckled

fingers. He stepped into the shallows and stared at the turbulent surface.

'Remember, let your eyes guide your hand,' his father said quietly behind him.

The boy let his vision unfocus until the river became a gray backdrop. An expectant hush fell around him, as if the world was holding its breath. He was wondering whether his father experienced the same feeling of detachment during a hunt when silver suddenly flashed to his left. His arm moved of its own volition.

The spear slipped into the water and found its prey.

The boy gaped. 'I did it. Father, I did it!'

He lifted the weapon and gazed proudly at the trout thrashing around on its sharp tip.

His father kissed his head and ruffled his hair. 'Well done, son. We shall have a nice supper this eve.'

The boy's father placed their catch in an oilskin bag and cleaned the weapons in the rapids while the boy hoisted the fishing cage sitting on the bank into his arms. Freshwater mussels rattled around the bottom. He turned and followed his father into the forest.

Giant evergreens rose around them as they trod the path their footsteps had carved into the land over the years. The branches of the trees were heavy with snow, their crowns almost invisible against the clear sky. Cones and needle-shaped leaves covered the ground and filled the air with the clean, fresh smell of sap.

Winter had come early to the mountains this year. The days started to grow short and the nights long several weeks ago, much to the boy's irritation.

He had had to wait until he was seven before his mother allowed him to accompany his father on his fishing and hunting trips. It wasn't until this summer, when he turned ten, that he received his very first hunting knife and spear. Just when he had started to get used to the weapons, he had woken up to the year's first snowfall.

His father pointed out plants and creatures as they navigated the trail home. The boy listened attentively. However many times they travelled this way, he always learned something new and fascinating. His enthusiasm dipped slightly when he was made to recite his French verbs. He stumbled over some of the words. His father corrected him gently and made him start all over again.

The boy did not begrudge this strict request. He knew his mind needed to be as strong as his body if he wanted to be even half the man his father was.

The smoky scent of burning wood reached them moments before the clearing appeared between the trees. A log cabin stood in the middle of the open circle of land. Although it wasn't big, the building was of sturdy construct and had withstood nine harsh winters in the desolate and unforgiving Carpathian Mountains.

The boy thought it was the best home that had ever existed in the whole wide world, especially since his father and mother had built it with their own hands when he was but a baby.

His father hastened his pace. The boy fell in behind him.

Seconds before they reached the porch, the front door opened and a woman stepped out. She had a large quilt in her hands and was using a stick to beat dust out of it. She paused and looked up at the sound of their footsteps.

'Mother, I did it! I caught a fish!' the boy shouted. He broke into a run and overtook his father.

A dazzling smile curved the woman's lips and lit her sparkling blue eyes. 'You did? Oh, that's wonderful!'

His father dropped the oilskin bag, scaled the shallow steps to the stoop, and lifted the woman by her waist. The stick and the quilt thudded to the porch. She gripped his shoulders and laughed wildly as he spun her around. He finally stopped and held her against him.

'Hello, wife,' he said softly, his gray eyes brimming with love.

'Hello, husband.' She lowered her head and kissed him. His arms tightened around her.

The boy grimaced. He had become accustomed to these displays over the years. Though he couldn't for the life of him fathom why pressing one's lips against another person's could make two people so happy, it evidently did, judging by the number of times his parents engaged in the activity.

He tolerated their passionate embrace for as long as he could before releasing a loud sigh.

His father reluctantly broke the kiss and slowly lifted his head. 'Our son is a villain intent on stopping our lovemaking,' he muttered.

His mother wrinkled her nose. 'I suspect you were the same at that age, love. Give it another five years. We will be beating females off him in droves.'

The boy listened to this conversation with an affronted air. 'I shall never kiss a girl. They are soft and— and horrid!'

His father threw back his head and laughed.

'Oh.' His mother's eyes narrowed. 'Are you calling me horrid?'

The boy opened and closed his mouth soundlessly.

'Come here! You shall be punished for such impudent words,' she said in a fake growl.

She was at his side in a heartbeat and raised him high in the air. The boy squealed and squirmed as she pressed her lips repeatedly to his face and neck, blowing ticklish raspberries into his skin.

'Stop! Stop, mother! Father, make her stop!' he gasped between giggles.

His father grinned and shook his head. 'You should know better by now, son.'

They had the fish and the remains of the vegetable stew from the day before for their supper. His mother helped him practice his written Latin while his father cleaned the rest of their catch before storing the fish with the mussels in the icebox under the kitchen floor. Later that night, the boy lay in bed and listened rapturously while his father told him a story. Though he had heard it many times before, he never grew tired of listening to the tales about two races of men who could survive death itself.

As he drifted off to sleep, the boy heard his mother stop in the doorway of his room.

'I fear the snow will only get heavier in the weeks to come,' she said quietly. 'You should go down to the village soon, before the passage becomes impassable.'

He heard his father murmur his accord.

The next morning, the boy woke to the sound of a muffled thud coming from the front of the cabin. His eyes widened. He slipped out of his bed and ran barefoot to the kitchen. His suspicion was confirmed when he saw what lay on the table.

'Father, can I come with you?' he asked eagerly, his gaze switching between the two adults who stood there.

His father looked up from the heavy, leather sack he was packing. He was already dressed in his thick winter coat and sturdy, fur-lined boots. He raised a questioning eyebrow at the woman across from him.

A frown creased her brow as she finished folding a pile of animal pelts into a second bag. She turned and pinned the boy with a narrow stare. He held his breath.

'I shall agree to let you accompany your father on one condition.'

The boy's heart sank. 'What condition is that?'

'That you shall learn the *basse danse* upon your return.'

The boy groaned while his father chortled.

'I am determined that at least one of the men in my life should be able to dance. Since your father is about as graceful as a duck on ice, this responsibility sadly falls to you,' his mother stated.

The boy hung his head and considered his options. There were not many of them.

'A duck on ice?' his father muttered.

'You make up for it in other ways, *mon cher*.'

The boy sighed. 'I will do it.'

They set off shortly after on the day-long journey that would take them east through the forests and the treacherous pass in the mountains to the neighboring valley. The boy could barely hide his excitement. He had only been to the village once before and was thrilled to be able to visit there again before winter confined them to the cabin.

It was an uneventful trip. They spent most of it going over the lessons he had learned the previous week and talking about the various plants and creatures they saw on their travel.

Dusk had covered the land in inky shadows when the lights of the village finally appeared in the distance below them. Nestled in the curve of a river, the commune of one hundred souls was the closest human outpost within walking distance of their home. His father travelled there twice a year to trade fur from the animals he hunted for oil and rare goods.

The boy studied the towering wall of solid timber that enclosed the settlement. *Fortification against invaders and looters,* his father had told him the first time he saw it. A creak echoed in the night as they turned the corner and came within sight of the gates. The entrance to the village was being secured.

'Hurry,' said his father. The boy quickened his step.

They slipped through the narrowing gap seconds before the portal thudded closed. His father greeted the two men in charge of the gateway.

'Haven't seen you in a long time,' one of them said with a grunt. His gaze dropped. 'Is this your boy? He has grown big.'

'That he has,' his father said in an even voice. 'Is there room at the inn, do you know?'

The man hawked and spat in the mud. 'Some passing tradesmen came through today.' He shrugged. 'You can always ask to be put up in one of the stables if they cannot lodge you there.'

His father expressed his thanks and wished the men a good evening.

A thin film of ice covered the puddles dotting the busy main thoroughfare, the glassy sheets amplifying the yellow glare from the torches and oil lamps lining the porches of shops. The boy peeked through open doorways and caught intriguing glimpses of a world he knew little of. Icy drops fell from the sky and struck his neck as he stumbled after his father. The boy shivered and looked up at the large, two-storey establishment they were headed for. Set apart from the other buildings, it stood at the top of a slope and towered over the rest of the village.

A few curses rose around them as people slipped in the dirty slush in their rush to find cover from the downpour. As they passed the smithy, a man missed his step and collided heavily with the boy's father. The stranger looked up, mumbled an apology, and moved out of their way.

A moment later, the boy felt a hot gaze on the back of his neck. He looked over his shoulder.

The man who had bumped into his father stood motionless in the middle of the street, oblivious to the rain pelting down from the heavens and the villagers scurrying around him. His pale face glistened in the light of the flickering flames from the smithy's forge as he stared at them.

The boy had opened his mouth to call out to his father when a loud crash sounded from up ahead, startling him. He bumped into the back of his father's legs, grabbed the reassuring weight of his winter coat, and peered around his waist.

A couple of men had staggered out of the inn's entrance. For a moment, the boy thought they were embracing. It did not take long to realize from their muffled grunts and red faces that they were, in fact, brawling. A thick stench of sweat and spirits washed over the boy and his father as they watched the two figures exchange clumsy blows. The men landed in the mud. They swatted at each other and were crawling onto their knees when a bucketful of dirty water hit them in the face. They choked and spluttered.

The boy stared at the full-bosomed figure who stood in the brightly-lit doorway, empty bucket in hand. It was the innkeeper's wife.

'And let that be a lesson to you, you rogues!' the woman snapped. 'Now, leave!'

The men gaped at her, climbed unsteadily to their feet, and tottered down the incline toward the village thoroughfare. By the time they reached the bottom, they had their arms wrapped around each other's waists for support.

The stranger who had stood staring after the boy and his father had disappeared.

'Oh.' The innkeeper's wife brightened when she saw them. She greeted the boy's father warmly.

'Come now, don't be frightened,' he murmured. The boy stepped out from behind his father's reassuring form and blinked in the light.

'Good Gods! This is never your son!' the woman exclaimed. 'What a handsome devil!'

To the boy's utter horror, the innkeeper's wife grabbed his shoulders and planted a big, fat, wet kiss on his cheek. He was still recovering from the shock of the experience when his father ushered him into the bustling, smoky interior of the building.

The next hours passed with dream-like swiftness. Since the inn also served as the village store, the boy watched his father exchange the animal pelts they had brought in their sacks for oil, sugar, spices, and other scarce merchandise they would need to survive the harsh winter in the mountains. As they ate a hearty meal with some of the tradesmen who were staying at the inn, the boy became aware of two girls staring at him from the landing at the top of the stairs. They giggled and whispered to each other whenever he looked their way. The boy saw the innkeeper's wife smile and wondered with a mild degree of panic whether he would have to suffer the ignominy of being kissed by her daughters as well before the night was over.

He was spared this fate when his father told him that it was time for bed. The innkeeper's wife had asked two of her guests to share a room so as to accommodate the boy and his father. Full of hot food and a suspiciously copious supply of free beer, the men had mumbled their wholehearted acquiescence to her request.

As he lay next to his father and let sleep claim him, the boy thought once more of the man who had watched them earlier that evening.

They made several purchases at the shops and craftsmen's houses in the village the next morning before heading through the open gates and into the mountains. A blizzard slowed their progress when they got to the pass and they did not reach home until late in the night.

The boy's mother took one look at them, got a bath ready in front of the roaring fire, and scrubbed them both to within an inch of their lives before sending them to bed. By the time the boy snuggled beneath his covers, he had all but forgotten about the stranger from the village.

The next day, his mother taught him the *basse danse*. He discovered that he was also as graceful as a duck on ice, much to his mother's horror and his father's everlasting amusement.

THEY CAME SHORTLY AFTER DAYBREAK, OVER A FORTNIGHT later.

The boy was collecting fresh kindling in the woods behind the cabin when the neighs of horses and the thuds of hooves pounding the ground interrupted him. He looked around with a frown.

There had only ever been a handful of visitors to his home in living memory. Most had been woodcutters attracted by the smoke spouting from the cabin chimney. The rest had been trappers and hunters who stayed in the shadows beneath the trees and passed by without exchanging a word.

The boy turned and headed back, curious as to who had brought horses so far in the wild. He had just come within sight of the clearing when he heard voices raised in anger.

A loud bang made him jump. He dropped the bundle of twigs he carried in his arms.

A scream blotted out the dying echoes of the boom.

The sound froze the boy's feet to the ground. It was his mother's voice. Then he was moving, his legs pumping through air that suddenly felt as thick as molasses. He passed the tree where he had left the wooden practice sword his father had carved for him from an oak branch, grabbed the weapon, and rounded the corner of the cabin. He skidded to a halt in the snow. His heart stuttered.

His father lay motionless in front of the porch. An ugly

wound distorted the area over his left breast. Blood pooled around the gaping crater and stained his shirt in an ever widening, crimson circle.

The boy's knees almost gave out beneath him. His father had been shot. He watched desperately for any movement of his chest or telltale pluming of air from his lips or nose. He saw none.

The boy's gaze darted to the figures on horseback who watched his father's still shape. There were six of them, men with polished features and refined clothing that looked out of keeping with the surrounding wilderness. Silver glinted in the bridles and saddles of their horses, giant beasts with gleaming coats and braided manes and tails.

A figure dashed out of the cabin. The boy's stomach lurched. It was his mother.

She held two blades in her hands. The boy recognized his father's broadsword and his mother's own rapier. She was at the bottom of the porch steps in a heartbeat and assumed a defensive stance in front of the unmoving figure on the ground.

'Please, don't do this,' she begged the silent men.

Someone laughed. The boy stared, horrified, as the man in the lead dismounted and approached his mother. His companions followed suit and unsheathed their swords. The boy's gaze dropped to the first man's waist. A sinister looking, round, metal object sat in a leather harness next to his scabbard. The boy recognized it as a matchlock pistol from his father's lessons on the art of war.

'Just tell the Council you didn't find us,' his mother

continued in a trembling voice. 'Please, Alexander, we haven't harmed any—'

'Silence!' the man yelled.

The boy's mother twitched.

'Do not take me for a fool!' the man called Alexander uttered in a sibilant whisper. 'You knew full well the sin you committed when you decided to lie with this traitorous Crovir snake, daughter of Bastian.' He kicked the boy's father in the leg. 'You lost the privileges of your station and the right to live the day you gave birth to that monster.' He paused and glared at the open doorway of the cabin. 'Where is that bastard half-breed of yours? Hiding like a dog, is he?'

The other men chuckled.

The boy's heart raced in fear and shock. Crovir and Bastian were the names of the immortal races from the tales his father had oft told him.

'Alexander, I'm begging you.' Tears streamed down his mother's ashen face. 'He is an innocent child. He does not—'

Her words were cut off by a backhanded slap that almost sent her tumbling to the ground. A trickle of blood escaped her nose and split lip as she steadied herself on the two blades.

A hot feeling flooded the boy's chest. These men had killed his father and hurt his mother. Before he knew it, he was charging from the tree line, an animal sound tearing up his throat as he raised his wooden sword in a double-handed grip.

His mother's eyes widened. 'No! *Run!*'

The boy landed two blows before someone kicked him in the stomach. He choked for air, stunned by the pain that paralyzed his breathing. His sword fell from his grasp. Fingers closed on his hair and pulled him up until he was practically on tiptoes. His scalp prickled where a few tendrils parted with his skin.

'*Aha!* Here is the mongrel!' someone spat in his face. It was the man called Alexander. Hate turned the man's eyes to smoldering coals. He smirked at the boy's mother. 'The tattletale who told us of your whereabouts said he seemed ordinary. Not much to look at, this runt of yours, is he, Catarine? Why, I could break his neck with my bare hands!' His grip tightened.

The boy blinked back tears as his father's killer yanked a handful of dark curls from his head. He suddenly recalled the stranger who had bumped into them in the village. He knew without a doubt that man was responsible for these people's presence at his home. The boy gritted his teeth, looked down, and grabbed the pistol from the man's waistband. The latter released him as he raised the weapon in shaking hands.

'Why, it seems we have a regular hero in the making here.' Alexander sneered. 'What will you do now, boy? Are you going to shoot us?'

A strange feeling of calmness descended upon the boy when he glanced at his mother's stricken expression. His grip steadied on the pistol. He would defend her at all costs.

He aimed the weapon at the grinning killer and pulled on the bottom lever.

There was a flare of sparks and a dry click. The pistol did not discharge.

The boy stared at it in dull incomprehension. Too late,

he remembered the lead shots that needed to be inserted in the barrel.

Alexander's mocking laughter echoed around the clearing. 'You stupid, stupid child! What did you think would—?' He broke off.

The boy had turned and cast the pistol as far as he could into the forest. There was a distant crash from among the trees.

'Why, you—' Alexander stormed toward him, his eyes deadly. The boy backed away.

A clash of metal stayed the man's stride. He looked over his shoulder toward the front of the cabin.

The boy blinked.

His father was up on his feet and fighting four of the men with his broadsword. The boy's mother stood close to him, her own blade slicing the air deftly as she engaged the fifth man.

The horses threw their heads back and snorted, hooves stamping the ground in agitation as they moved away.

Alexander turned on his heels and drew his sword.

'Father,' the boy whispered numbly.

His father was alive. Yet, he had been so sure that he had died.

The boy's mother yelled his name, startling him. He grabbed his wooden sword and slipped around the fighting figures to the cover of the porch. An ill-matched battle unfolded before him while he watched with bated breath, knuckles white on the handle of his sword. A wave of heat washed over his back from the open doorway behind him. He whirled around and ran inside the cabin.

His frantic gaze scoured the room and found what he

sought. He grabbed the hunting knives from the table next to the wash bucket and raced back outside.

'*Catarine!*' his father bellowed.

The boy rocked to a stop. Air froze on his lips. His limbs went slack. The weapons clattered onto the porch.

A blade had found his mother's skin. Her attacker yanked his sword out of her body in a slashing motion. She gasped and clamped a hand to the gaping wound in her abdomen. Blood gushed from under her fingers.

She looked at the boy's father with a dazed expression. 'Balthazar,' she breathed.

'Stand back!' he barked. Sweat beaded his face despite the cold and his chest heaved with his breathing. Crimson trails laced his arms from several cuts.

Two of his attackers lay in the snow, dead from dreadful lacerations carved into their bodies.

The boy's mother staggered toward the porch. The boy leapt down the steps and caught her as she fell. He looped his arms around her body and pressed his hands to her wound. Hot scarlet stained his fingers, the flow pulsing with her slowing heartbeat. Her pale face blurred in the swell of tears that filled his vision.

She grabbed his hand and whispered, 'I love you.'

A low sob escaped him when he felt her go limp. He stared into her open, unblinking eyes, shivers racking his body.

The boy's father froze in the midst of swinging his blade. Horror clouded his gray gaze. He roared and redoubled his efforts to push back their attackers.

Alexander's sword slashed across the side of his neck a moment later.

'*Father!*' the boy shrieked.

His father thudded to his knees, a hand clasped to the red jet spurting from his throat. Sorrow filled his face as he looked around at the boy and the dead woman lying in his lap.

'I love you, son.' He collapsed forward in the snow. His eyes fluttered closed.

A loud ringing sounded in the boy's ears.

'No,' he mumbled. He stared from his father to his mother. His voice rose to a shrill scream of denial. '*Nooooo!*'

There was motion in the clearing. The men his father had slain were slowly rising to their feet.

'You did not know?'

The boy's numb gaze moved from the two figures to Alexander's face.

The man appeared to be relishing something. 'They never told you, did they? I cannot believe it!' He sneered. 'Oh, you are going to *enjoy* what is still to come, boy! This delicious farce is far from over!'

The boy watched him wordlessly, unable to grasp his meaning.

Two men rolled his father's body over. 'Do you want to finish him off now?' one of them asked. He held a blade over the dead man's neck.

Alexander's gaze did not shift from the boy's face. 'No. Let him rise and fight again. I want this mongrel to witness what is going to happen next.'

The men glanced at each other, their expressions uneasy. 'The Hunters' code forbids us from—'

'The Hunters' code be damned!' Alexander snapped. 'Our names will be engraved in immortal history for killing these two traitors and the evil they birthed!' Spittle flew from his mouth and his shoulders heaved with angry breaths.

A shudder ran through the body in the boy's arms. He looked down in time to see his mother's eyes blink open. Horror numbed his senses as the reality of what he had witnessed and heard finally sank in.

His parents were immortals. As were the men who had come to slaughter them.

In the hours that followed, Alexander's threat became a harrowing truth that seared the boy's mind and forever shattered his innocence.

His father rose from death eight times more and raised his blade to defend all that he loved with every fibre of his being. When his final breath left his body and he lay unmoving on the frozen ground, a crow cawed shrilly from a nearby tree.

Two men held the boy back while the others took turns killing his mother another sixteen times. They stood patiently over her and waited until she showed signs of life before stabbing her savagely in the heart.

Before her seventeenth and final death, the boy's mother managed to turn her head and look at him for the last time. She mouthed a single word.

A second crow joined the first one, its wings rustling loudly in the silence that followed.

The boy's mouth opened on a cry that came out as a whisper. His throat was raw and his voice hoarse from his screams.

Alexander collected the wooden sword from the porch. 'I am curious to see what you can do, boy. Here, use this to defend yourself.' He threw the weapon at the boy's feet.

The other men exchanged troubled looks.

'Alexander, this has gone far enough,' one of them said in a warning tone. 'Our orders were to kill them, not—not torment them like this! Let us be done.'

Alexander ignored the speaker. 'Let him go,' he said silkily to the men holding the boy.

They released him reluctantly.

'Pick it up.'

The boy looked dazedly at the wooden sword.

'*Pick it up!*' Alexander shouted.

The boy lunged and grabbed the sword. His body shook uncontrollably. He cast beseeching glances at the other men. They did not meet his eyes.

A silver blade hummed past the boy's face. He stumbled backward.

Metal clanged against wood. The boy stared from the wooden sword he had automatically raised to Alexander's surprised expression.

The boy fended off another two blows before the man's sword found his arm. He cried as heat carved a path along his skin from elbow to wrist. Blood dripped onto the snow.

A hand closed around his throat. Alexander lifted him with one hand. The boy thrashed and kicked, blood roaring in his ears as he wheezed against the iron vice choking air from his lungs. The man watched him struggle for timeless seconds before slamming him down on the ground.

Pain exploded through the boy's back and head as he made contact with the frozen ground.

A crushing weight landed on his right hand. He heard

bone pop. Alexander ground his boot into his fingers and raised his sword in both hands.

The boy's terrified gaze focused on the gleaming tip as it descended toward him. The blade pierced the skin over his heart and entered his body in a single, savage thrust.

He gasped. Numbness flared from the wound and spread through his entire being. Tears streamed silently down his face as he gazed at Alexander's triumphant expression. The boy felt his heart slow. A circle of darkness encroached on his vision. As his awareness dimmed and his eyes flickered closed, he thought he heard the sound of approaching hoofbeats and someone shout his name.

The sun had passed its zenith when he awoke. The boy blinked at the snow falling from the gray, winter skies and the dark shadows moving between the white flakes.

Crows circled the clearing, a giant swarm that blocked out half the heavens. But for the crackling of their wings, the birds were silent.

The boy lay frozen for a long time as he waited for a blade to sink into his heart once more. When none came, he pushed himself up and looked around. He breathed in sharply.

The birds perched on the roof of the cabin and the branches of nearby trees. They dotted the blood-stained ground and sat docilely on the eight bodies around him.

Horror brought a flood of bile to the boy's mouth. He ignored the throbbing from his injuries, leapt to his feet, and swung his wooden sword clumsily at the crows resting on his mother and father.

'Go away!' he yelled.

The birds hopped out of the way of the blade before returning to the bodies. The boy's eyes rounded when he studied the other figures and recognized the men who had come to kill them. An ugly grimace distorted Alexander's face in death. Stab wounds and slashes covered his frame. The boy's gaze moved to the tree line. He spotted three of the horses beneath the snow-laden branches.

A sudden downdraft pushed against him. He looked up and stared, appalled, as flock upon flock of black shapes descended from the sky and covered the motionless figures on the ground. The horses startled and galloped away, alarmed snorts fading into the distance.

The boy made several attempts to rid his parents' bodies of the sinister creatures, to no avail. Although he expected the crows to peck and gore the corpses beneath them, they did no such thing. Instead, they shrouded the bodies with their wings, their coal black eyes almost sad as they watched him.

He had no forewarning of their departure. In a single motion that seemed to denote some kind of silent communication, the birds left just as suddenly as they had appeared, a vast cloud of fluttering wings that darkened the clearing.

In the stead of the bodies were eight discrete piles of ashes. Some flakes fluttered onto the snow.

The boy choked and dropped to his knees by his parents' remains. He tried to gather the precious mounds in his hands even as a bluster of wind coursed through the clearing and scattered the gray specks.

'No,' he whispered, frozen fingers clutching desperately at the vanishing grains of earthly dust that were all that was left of his mother and father.

A noise brought his head up. His stomach lurched. He stared at the trees to his left.

There was no one there.

The boy studied the shadows in the forest intently. He could not help but feel that he was being watched. His gaze finally returned to where his parents had lain.

There was nothing left of their ashes.

Hot tears scalded the boy's cheeks. His shoulders sagged. He remained still for a long time before leaning down and kissing the ground where his parents had lain. He closed his eyes and said a short prayer before staggering to his feet.

Cold determination filled his veins. He knew what he had to do.

The boy collected the hunting knives from the porch and entered the cabin. He cleaned the wounds on his chest and arm and wrapped a roll of fresh linen tightly around them. Next, he packed a bag with food, a full waterskin, several rolls of clean linen, a tinderbox, and a spare change of clothes. He shrugged into his winter coat, put on a second layer of socks, and pulled his boots back on. He slipped the hunting knives inside his pockets.

The boy doused the fire and walked slowly around the place he had called his home for as long as he had lived. Tears threatened to fill his eyes again when he stood in the doorway of his parents' room. He wiped at them angrily and stormed out of the cabin, the bag strapped to his back.

He stopped on the steps and sat down. He stared at his right hand.

His fingers were swollen and bruised where Alexander had stamped on his hand. Two were misshapen.

He had seen his father suffer a similar injury before and recalled what he had done.

The boy swallowed convulsively. He lay a roll of linen next to him, found a thick stick, and gripped it between his teeth. He took a few deep breaths, grabbed the first angled finger, and yanked on it sharply.

A muffled scream escaped his throat as he bit down on the wood. He rocked and hugged his hand to his chest, silent sobs coursing through him. He waited but a moment before repeating the action with the second finger.

This time, the stick snapped in half in his mouth.

Once the pain dulled, the boy wrapped the linen around the two fingers and strapped them to a third one. He rose to his feet, descended the last step, and headed into the forest without looking back.

His destination was a village in a valley two mountains and at least three days' walk away. He had never been there before and had only heard his father speak of it once. It seemed a safer place to go than the settlement he had recently visited.

He walked until dusk fell and found shelter in a hollow formed by three giant boulders on the slope of the mountain. He gathered kindling and wood before lighting a fire. He slept fitfully that night, his dreams plagued by images of blood and death. When morning came, he discovered that the injuries on his hand and arm had almost healed. The wound on his chest still stung.

He also found a cluster of prints in the snow a short distance from where he had been resting.

Unease filtered through the boy as he studied the distinctly shaped impressions. He had seen them before, in the three years that he had gone hunting with his father.

They were wolves' tracks.

His eyes darted to the murky spaces between the trees. If the animals had been around before, they were not there now. A strange feeling crept over him. Once more, he felt like he was being watched. He scrutinized the landscape for a long time before setting off briskly toward the west.

He heard the first howl as evening came, just after he crossed the first peak. By then, the boy was convinced he was being stalked. He found an abandoned den at the base of a giant evergreen moments before a sudden snowstorm swept across the mountain. He kept a large fire burning brightly for most of that night and hardly slept; every rustle, crackle, and hiss jolted him awake to peer in panic at shadowy shapes that never materialized into anything.

He set out early the next day. He had barely travelled fifty feet from the den when he saw the paw prints once more. They had increased in number.

The sun had crossed the halfway point above his head when he came to a river at the bottom of the valley. It was not much larger than the one where he had often fished with his father. He refilled his waterskin, examined the rapids, and walked upstream until he found a safe passage across the water. Snow started to fall again when he was midway over.

He was wading out of the shallows on the other side when a baying close by sent a shiver down his spine and froze his legs. The boy looked back and saw the first dark shape appear on the opposite bank. Others followed.

There were eight of them in all.

The wolves stood and watched him silently through a thin veil of snow.

The boy's heart slammed a wild beat against his chest. He turned and ran into the forest as fast as his legs could carry him.

Splashes sounded behind him as the wolves dove into the water. It would take them less than a minute to reach his side of the river.

As the boy crashed through the undergrowth, mouth dry with fear, he listened out for the sound of the pack closing in. A dim commotion rose above the rush of blood in his ears. He heard echoes of distant growls and some loud yelps.

It was another hour before he felt safe enough to stop.

By then, sweat had soaked through his clothes and his socks. He built a fire and stood shivering in his winter coat and boots while he dried them; he knew all too well the perils of wet clothing in this kind of weather. He did not linger once he dressed himself and headed swiftly for the foothills of the second mountain.

Twilight came all too soon and with it no sign of the snowfall abating. The boy decided to continue walking into the night. With any luck, he might reach the village by the morning.

But fortune was not with him that eve.

As clouds blanketed the moon and the stars, rendering the darkness almost complete, howls broke out behind him. The boy rocked to a standstill and whirled around. This time, he did not imagine the noise of paws striking the ground and bodies plowing through brushwood.

He turned and bounded into the forest. Although he now knew he was an immortal who had survived his first death, he did not know what would happen if he ended up in the stomachs of several hungry creatures.

It was minutes before he spotted the first wolf. Its gray coat danced between the white flakes some twenty feet to his left. He looked around and saw four more shapes close on his trail.

Terror flooded the boy's body. A whimper passed his lips.

His mother's face suddenly flashed before his eyes. He remembered the last word she had breathed to him before she passed.

Live.

An angry resolve replaced his fear. The boy looked ahead and quickened his step, aware that to fall would be fatal. He slipped his fingers inside his left coat pocket and pulled out one of the hunting knives and a piece of linen. He gripped the weapon so that the blade faced down and wrapped the linen tightly around his fist, securing it to his hand. He used his mouth and repeated the process with the second knife and his right hand.

If he was to die here tonight, he would not go down without a fight.

A giant evergreen appeared up ahead. The boy's eyes rose to its thick branches. A wild thought formed in his mind.

He heard a snarl and a snap of jaws at his heels.

The boy raced for the tree and jumped a couple of seconds before he reached it. Time seemed to slow as he drifted weightlessly through the air and brought his arms up.

He had timed his leap correctly.

The knives stabbed into the trunk at the peak of his rise. He pulled his knees up almost instantly to his chest.

Something snagged at his coat's tail just as his feet landed safely against the tree, his thighs gripping the bark. A heavy weight dragged him down. Barks and growls filled the space beneath him. The boy looked over his shoulder, saw the wolf's gleaming eyes, and kicked him in the snout.

The animal yelped but did not let go.

A snarl not dissimilar to the wolves' own angry sounds tore through the boy's throat. He kicked again.

The wolf dropped back in the snow.

Quick as lightning, the boy scaled the tree, using the knives as grips. He found a bough thick enough to bear his weight some twenty feet above the ground and straddled it before hugging the trunk. Shivers shook his limbs and his heart pounded wildly in his chest.

The wolves danced around the base of the evergreen, disappointment evident in their whines and growls. They stayed for some time before wandering off a short distance.

The snowfall doubled in the following hour. Gusts of icy wind howled down the mountain and brought sleet. The wolves remained where they were.

The boy thrust the knives into the tree to moor

himself and leaned tiredly into the trunk. He would have to stay there that night. He had no other choice.

Sometime later, the boy thought he heard a disturbance above the noise of the storm. He peered into the thick, gray curtain of icy rain and snow to where the wolves had been but could see nothing.

Although he had thought he would not be able to sleep, the boy was stunned to see bright sunlight when he blinked and next opened his eyes.

The blizzard had abated and a heavy silence surrounded him. A thick carpet of pristine snow covered everything in sight, muting the sounds of the forest. He looked down and saw no fresh tracks beneath the tree.

The wolves had disappeared.

The boy climbed down warily, stopping every few feet or so to inspect his surroundings before he reached the ground. He drank some water, ate a handful of dried berries, and set off once more.

He passed the second peak uneventfully and started his descent into the next valley before the sun had reached its midday point. He came to a river a couple of hours later and followed it downstream.

As he rounded a curve in the land, he saw wisps of smoke curling above the treetops in the distance.

The boy almost started crying then.

He had reached the village.

Fortifications appeared as he drew closer. Although the settlement looked smaller than the one he had visited more than a fortnight earlier, it looked well-kept. He climbed the bank of the river until he reached a slush-covered track. He was about to start down it when the back of his neck prickled.

The boy turned. Something moved in the tree line some fifty feet along the path. He blinked.

For a moment, he thought he saw the form of a man. He scrutinized the silent forest for almost a minute before he convinced himself he had imagined it.

He set off once more and followed the road toward the solid timber wall visible between the trees ahead.

A man stood guarding the village gates. He watched the boy's approach with a frown.

'Do you travel alone?' he asked suspiciously when the boy came within earshot.

The boy stopped. He swallowed and nodded.

'Where are your parents?'

'They are—my parents are dead!' the boy stammered.

The man's eyes widened. 'Good Gods! From what?' He stiffened and drew himself up, eyes narrowing. 'Were they afflicted with illness?'

The boy shook his head. 'No. They were—' He paused and racked his head for a plausible explanation. One presented itself readily. 'They were killed by wolves.'

The man swore. He gazed at the boy for a stunned moment, his face waxen.

'Come, I shall take you somewhere safe,' he mumbled.

The boy followed him through the gates. His gaze darted sideways as they navigated a path through a maze of one-storey buildings. Men, women, and children went about their daily business around him. Although some bestowed curious looks upon him, none seemed hostile or called him a monster.

The man instructed someone to guard the gates before leading the boy to a large structure at the end of a winding trail. As his gaze swept over the chimneys in the slanted rooftop, the boy guessed that this was the village inn. He headed inside after the man and stood nervously by the door while his guide conversed in hushed tones with the giant figure behind the counter. He was aware of the dim shapes of other men watching him in the light of the flames flickering in the hearth to the right.

A wave of exhaustion suddenly swept over the boy. The horrific, life-changing events of the last few days were finally catching up with him. He almost collapsed to his knees there and then.

The innkeeper shouted for someone at the rear of the building. A door opened and a woman bustled out of what looked to be a kitchen. Her belly was swollen with child and she wiped her hands briskly on an apron. She stopped by the counter and listened to the two men while they spoke in low voices.

Her hand rose to her lips, her eyes flaring. She dipped her head at the innkeeper, her gaze never leaving the boy's face. She crossed the floor and slowly lowered herself on her heels before him.

'My name is Ioana,' she said in a soft voice. 'I am the mistress of this house. Mihai told us what happened to your family.' She indicated the man who had been guarding the village gates. 'Do you have relatives, an uncle or aunt maybe who could care for you?'

The boy's eyes prickled hotly. He shook his head.

His parents had never spoken to him of any siblings or even grandparents.

'Oh.' Pity and sadness flashed in the woman's eyes. She chewed her lip and watched him for a silent moment. Her gaze dropped to her belly. She patted the bump thoughtfully. 'You know, with the baby due soon, I had hoped to find someone to help me around here for a bit,' she hazarded.

The boy registered the unspoken invitation on the face of the innkeeper's wife before looking past her shoulder at the enormous figure behind the counter.

The innkeeper shrugged at the same time that Ioana muttered, 'Oh, never mind him. My husband will do as he is told. So, what say you?'

The boy gulped past the sudden lump in his throat. 'Yes,' he whispered.

'Good,' Ioana said with a brisk nod. 'Now, help me up and I will show you to your room. You look about ready to drop dead.'

The boy assisted the innkeeper's wife to her feet and fell in step behind her.

She stopped suddenly and turned. 'I almost forgot. What is your name, child?'

The boy hesitated for a heartbeat. 'My name is Lucas.'

THE END

DANCING BLADES

A SEVENTEEN SERIES SHORT STORY

A.D. STARRLING

The katana hummed through the air, its curved edge heading inexorably toward my chest. I dove to the side. Wisps of black drifted from my temple where the sword sliced through my hair. Cries erupted from the crowd gathered in the fish market, shock and delight displayed in equal measure on the faces of the spectators.

I landed on my back with a harsh grunt.

A sandaled foot stamped on my right wrist before I could move. The man looming above me kicked at the sword in my hand. It skittered across the cobbled square and came to rest at the feet of a wide-eyed little boy. He leaned down to touch it but was yanked away by his anxious mother before his fingers could make contact with the metal.

Something sharp dented the skin at the base of my throat. I froze and stared past the gleaming, steel edge of the katana at my attacker's inscrutable face.

'Do you submit?' he said calmly.

I studied the man for a moment, admiration darting through me despite the sword pressed against my neck.

Dressed in dark blue hakama trousers and a grey hitatare vest, Musashi Miyamoto cut an impressive figure even for a samurai. Taller than most of his countrymen by a good few inches, he had a broad physique and sinewy arms that spoke of his skills as a martial artist and swordsman. Dark strands had escaped his topknot and framed his rugged face, giving him a wild look.

I smiled faintly. 'Yes, I do. It still does not change the fact that I want you to be my teacher, Miyamoto-dono.'

He frowned. Although none deserved to be called a master more than he, Musashi was a modest man and loath to be seen as anything other than a humble warrior. It was one of the things I liked about him.

A figure moved behind the samurai. I glanced at the young boy who stood watching us with a grimace.

'Greetings, Iori-kun,' I said lightly to Musashi's adopted son.

Iori Miyamoto narrowed his eyes. 'I would appreciate it if you would not address me in such a familiar fashion, you crazy *nanbanjin*.'

I grinned; I had gotten used to being called a "southern barbarian" ever since I landed at the Port of Nagasaki a few months ago. Despite the fact that I now dressed like the locals and had grasped their complex language, there was no disguising my Caucasian features and blue eyes.

This was the fifth time I had challenged Musashi to a fight since I arrived in Japan. It was the fifth time I had lost to the great man. I voiced the same request I had made on the previous occasions I had faced him.

'Let me be your apprentice.'

Musashi sighed. 'No.'

JULY 1625. OSAKA. JAPAN.

CARTS RATTLED ACROSS THE WOODEN BRIDGE SPANNING THE river, another noise among the myriad others rising from the bustling streets behind me. The gates and turrets of an imposing castle towered against the skyline to the south, its forbidding stone walls marking the low hill that formed the center of the sprawling metropolis.

It had taken me just over a day to travel here from Kyoto. I had followed the Uji River as it meandered through the flatlands of the Yamashiro Basin and spent the night at an inn in one of the villages dotting the green valley. Although the innkeeper observed me with a healthy dose of suspicion, he did not turn me away. A dawn mist still hung over the rice fields when I departed the hamlet this morning, an uninterrupted vista of ghostly grey stretching out to the mountains to the west.

I leaned against the bridge railing and watched the riverboats crisscrossing the wide waterway below.

Like Nagasaki, Fukuoka, Nagoya, and Edo, Osaka made for an impressive port city. As an immortal who had travelled half the world, I could see why the islands of Japan held such a strong appeal for the Europeans wishing to expand their trading routes to the Pacific, foremost among them the increasingly powerful Dutch East India Company.

Splashes of color drew my gaze to the wharfs and docks lining the closest bank. Dyed banners and painted lanterns dotted the walls and terraces of the houses and shops crowding the water's edge. I had been told of the upcoming Tenjin Matsuri by the Kyoto merchant who gave me directions to Osaka. An annual festival dating back over eight hundred years to the Heian period, the Tenjin Matsuri was dedicated to a local patron god of learning and art and was apparently celebrated with great zeal by the Osakans over a period of two days.

I had a good feeling about the upcoming festivities. I could not help but sense that my long-held goal of becoming Musashi Miyamoto's apprentice was finally within reach. Of course, I had been wrong about that before.

After my fifth defeat at Musashi's hands in Edo nine months ago, I had shadowed the Miyamotos while they travelled across Japan as part of the samurai's ongoing *musha shugyō*, a warrior pilgrimage similar to that undertaken by medieval knights to prove their chivalry. I challenged the man to a duel four more times and lost every single one of those matches.

'This is becoming a tedious routine, Soul-san,' said Musashi the last time we fought. The man thrust his sword into the scabbard in his belt and folded his arms across his chest. 'Why do you still choose to pursue this hopeless dream? Most people would have given up after their first defeat.'

I wiped my bloodied lips and pressed a hand against the shallow cut he had inflicted on my shoulder.

'I am not most people, Miyamoto-dono. Besides, your reputation precedes you. You are one of the greatest sword masters alive in the world today. As such, I want you to teach me all that you know.'

Musashi frowned. 'Why? What is it that you wish to achieve with these skills?'

I hesitated. 'I want to learn how to survive the battles that will come my way.'

Musashi had watched me warily then. For the first time since I met him, I felt he had glimpsed my unearthly nature.

I was born in Prague in 1560, the half-breed son of a Bastian and a Crovir, two races of immortals who have walked the Earth since the dawn of mankind and possess the capacity to survive sixteen deaths. Two races forbidden from union that might result in offspring deemed an abomination.

Knowing I carried a death-sentence from the moment of my conception, my parents fled the immortal societies and hid from the men assigned to execute me. Shortly after my tenth birthday, they finally tracked us down. That day, the Hunters murdered my father and mother before my very eyes and I suffered my first death. How I escaped further deaths and survived remains a mystery to me.

It was several decades before I realized that I would not be able to escape my fate as the most hunted immortal in the world for much longer. With that in mind, I set out to hone my fighting skills in my own version of a warrior's pilgrimage.

I first heard of Musashi Miyamoto when I was traveling through China. Fascinated by the tales of the samurai who had never lost a single duel and who had conceived a deadly two-sword fighting style known as the Hyoto Niten Ichi-ryu, I came to Japan with a view to learning this new art from the man himself.

I frowned at the dark waters below. So far, my attempts at convincing Musashi to take me on as a student had failed miserably. I had not taken into account the complex nature of the man; that and the fact that he was as stubborn as a mule when it came to his custom of not taking on disciples he deemed unfit to train.

A voice interrupted my contemplation. I looked up from the busy riverscape.

'Would you like some *choboyaki*, friend?' said a wizened old man with a toothless smile.

I studied the steaming, grilled batter balls in the street vendor's two-wheeled pushcart. My stomach rumbled. The old man's grin widened.

I recalled what the man in Kyoto had told me about the inhabitants of Osaka. According to him, they were friendly, laid-back, free spirits with the single-minded focus of cut-throat merchants.

'Your status as a foreigner will mean nothing to them as long as you show the color of your coins,' he had said.

He was proved right when I became the happy owner of six choboyaki balls a moment later.

'Some sake?' said the old man. He uncorked a clay bottle.

The strong smell of fermented rice hit my nostrils.

I glanced at the late morning sun. 'A bit early for sake, is it not?'

The old man tut-tutted. 'It is never too early for sake, young man. 'Specially if this is your first time to our fair city.'

I ignored the "young man" comment, pulled more coins from the money pouch secured to my belt, and accepted the small cup of warm alcohol he handed me. At the ripe age of sixty-five, I still had the appearance of an eighteen-year-old.

'By the way, where would be the best place to find samurais here?' I asked, casually downing the drink.

The old man cocked his head to the side and observed me with a shrewd expression, his rheumy gaze flicking briefly to the katana at my waist.

'The samurai quarters are to the east of the city, stranger-san.' He paused. 'Are you looking for anyone in particular?'

'Yes. I seek a man by the name of Musashi Miyamoto.'

The toothless grin returned.

'You're in luck,' the street vendor said with some glee. 'He happens to be staying at the castle.' He indicated something over my shoulder with a tilt of his chin.

My heart sank. I turned and stared at the rooftops of the extensive fortress on the other side of the river.

'*That* castle?'

The old man nodded. I swore. He chuckled, uttered a parting, and wheeled his pushcart across the bridge.

I stood and frowned at the formidable towers in the distance.

It had been two months since I lost the Miyamotos' trail in Nagoya. Although I wanted to believe it was an accident, something told me that Musashi had finally gotten tired of the unwanted thorn plaguing his side. I suspected Iori had had some say in the matter as well.

Challenging Musashi to a duel in the middle of a public arena was one thing; getting into one of the most guarded castles in the country to do so was a completely different undertaking. I needed a plan to reach the man whom I wanted as my teacher. One that did not involve getting decapitated for being a suspected foreign spy.

I spent the rest of the day walking around the fifteen or so acres of land and the outer moat inside which the estate was built. After studying the formidable seventy-foot stone walls, thick metal gates, and well-staffed guardhouses protecting the castle, I came to the conclusion that I would lose several lives attempting to break into it. That left me only one choice. I was going to have to approach Musashi when he came out of the stone fortress.

It was to be several days before such an opportunity presented itself.

After taking up residence at a public inn in the merchant quarters to the north of the city, I found a good place opposite the west side of the outer moat from which I could observe the foot traffic in and out of the castle. Not long after I got there, on the fourth morning of my arrival in the metropolis, a large group of men set up makeshift tables under some cherry trees on the bank some thirty feet from where I stood and started to play shogi, the game of Japanese chess. I watched them for a while before returning to my daily routine of monitoring the gates.

It was mid afternoon when I spied a familiar figure strolling over the moat bridge.

'Hello, Iori-kun.'

Iori slowed when he saw me walk out of the shadow of a clump of trees.

'Oh good gods,' he muttered with all the aggravation a fourteen-year-old could muster.

He ignored me as I fell into step beside him. We headed into the city, an awkward silence falling between us.

'Where's your father?'

Iori remained resolutely mute. I glanced at the money pouch next to his bokken, the wooden training sword Musashi had given him.

'Off to buy some goods?'

Iori cast a blistering glare my way. I smiled. This seemed to infuriate him further.

I accompanied him as he negotiated the busy streets, curious as to what Musashi had asked the young man to purchase. To my surprise, in addition to stopping at food stalls, he also visited craft shops and bought a selection of ink sticks, washi paper, and some calligraphy brushes.

'Does your father paint?'

For a moment, it looked like Iori would not answer. 'Yes,' he finally admitted. 'It is part of his bushidō.'

I was familiar with the concept of the "Way of the Warrior," the moral code by which Japanese samurais lived. I had not realized that Musashi ascribed such importance to the artistic element of its virtues.

Iori glanced at me, as if sensing my unspoken question. 'There are many paths to the Way.'

Twilight was casting shadows across the land when we made our way back to the castle gates.

I stopped on the moat bridge and handed the young man the packages I had helped him carry. 'Will you let your father know that I wish to see him?'

Iori frowned. 'Are you going to challenge him to a duel again?'

I grimaced. 'Maybe.'

'Then, no.'

I sighed. 'What will it take for him to take me on as his apprentice?'

Iori looked down his nose at me, an admirable feat considering I towered over him by a foot and a half. 'In your case, a miracle.'

'Iori?' I called out as he headed inside the fortress.

'What?' he snapped over his shoulder.

'Tell your father I have all the time in the world.'

I waited until he disappeared from view before turning to walk back to the river. I allowed my gaze to wander naturally to the men playing shogi and spied the three figures who had followed Iori and me into the city.

One of them soon fell into step behind me. I stopped in several shops on my way to the inn where I was staying, my pace leisurely and designed to inspire confidence in the man shadowing me. He was very good at masking his aura. Had I been an ordinary man, his presence would have gone undetected.

Although he watched the public house where I had taken up residence for a good hour after I entered the building, the spy failed to notice me when I myself trailed him to a private house in the samurai quarters. I examined the layout of the two-storey building for a long time before returning to my living quarters and retiring for the evening.

The next few days followed the same pattern. Iori would come out of the castle in the afternoon on some errand for his father or one of the other resident samurais, and I accompanied him on his travels. Although he sported cuts and bruises from his training sessions, the young man never complained or showed any discomfort. He grew more relaxed in my presence and remained oblivious to the men who stalked us everyday.

Though I had my suspicions about what the men were after, it wasn't until the night before the Tenjin Matsuri that I finally gleaned the finer details of their scheme. By then, I had learned their routine and knew they would be relaxing in the hot pool in the garden after their evening meal.

It took but a moment for me to scale a tree next to the fence and drop silently inside the lush gardens surrounding the house. By the time the men came out to sit in the steaming water, I had been lying in the bushes next to the pool for a good half an hour.

'As we suspected, Musashi and Iori intend to partake of the local festivities with the Osaka Castle daimyo,' said the man whom I suspected to be the leader of the gang. 'If all goes according to plan, Musashi will be delayed for half an hour on the second evening and Iori will depart for the riverside after the lord's entourage has left the estate. It will be the ideal time to snatch the boy. The darkness and the crowds should mask any resistance he may offer.' He paused, an ugly expression dawning on his face. 'It will also be easy to dispose of that annoying *nanbanjin* who has been loitering around him.'

The annoying *nanbanjin* stayed deathly still for another hour while his would-be killers drank sake and talked about what they would do with the substantial ransom they intended to extract from Musashi and the feudal lords who favored the samurai. That Iori would be executed before any such sum was paid became all too painfully clear. For money was only their secondary aim.

It was almost midnight by the time I returned to the public house. By then, I had come to a decision as to the wisest course of action. I borrowed the necessary writing material I required from the innkeeper and clumsily composed a short letter to Musashi. Learning to speak Japanese was one thing; writing it was doubly hard. Finally satisfied with the gist of the message I had penned out, I took the missive to the castle. The guards eyed me coolly as I approached the gates. Thanks to my constant presence around Iori over the last week, they knew me by sight.

'Can you give this to Miyamoto-dono?' I said politely.

The guard I had spoken to looked at the paper as if it were a snake.

'It is an urgent matter,' I added with a weak smile.

The guard glanced at his companion. The latter shrugged in a "he-talked-to-you-first, this-is-now-your-problem" kind of way. The guard took the sealed letter between two fingers and disappeared inside the castle grounds. I waited patiently for his return. He reappeared an hour later.

'Miyamoto-dono wishes me to pass on his gratitude,' he said with a stiff nod.

I looked past his shoulder, expecting to see the samurai. Silent seconds passed. There was no sign of Musashi.

'Is that it?' I said.

The guard nodded.

'He is not coming out?'

The guard nodded again and indicated that I should leave.

I frowned as I walked back to the inn. *What was Musashi thinking? Did he read the message correctly?*

I spent a sleepless night pondering what the samurai intended to do about the group of mercenaries hell-bent on kidnapping his son. When morning came, I was still no clearer as to his potential countermove. I had given Musashi details of the men's location and expected him to have arrested them with the help of the lord of Osaka Castle. But when I headed into the samurai quarters to check on the house, it looked as peaceful as when I had left it the previous night.

The celebrations for the Tenjin Matsuri started early that day. After paying their respects at the shinto shrine dedicated to the festival god, the Osakans filled the streets of the city. Tantalizing smells and smoke soon clouded the air from the many food stalls lining the crowded passages, canals, and bridges. The beats of percussion drums and the cries from outdoor theatre performances competed with the locals in full vocal flow, creating a deafening wall of sound that should have raised the dead from their graves. The street processions of the daytime were followed by energetic music and dancing that carried on well into the evening.

I saw Iori and Musashi only from a distance. The feudal lord's escort was extensive and none could breach the solid wall of guards around it.

The second day of the festival was busier and louder than the first. A portable shrine occupied the midst of a noisy parade of chanting and cheering locals that moved slowly through the city, pulling in spectators along the way. Colorful giant lanterns and flame torches dotted the streets and waterways as evening fell and the growing crowds gradually converged upon the bridges and banks of the Okawa River. There, boat processions, bonfires, and a night-time fireworks performance would herald the end of the festivities.

The Osaka Castle daimyo left his estate at dusk. The Miyamotos were not among his entourage. I stood frowning in the shadows opposite the moat well after the last guards had crossed the bridge while I contemplated what to do next.

Is that Musashi's plan? He's intending to simply not show up?

If that was the case, then I could not intervene in good faith and engage the men intent on seizing Iori.

I was about to leave when I saw the younger Miyamoto appear at the gates. He was alone. My heart sank. I intercepted him when he crossed the moat.

'Where is your father?'

Iori looked somewhat relieved to see me. 'He has been detained by an urgent matter.'

I muttered something rude under my breath. 'Did he get the letter I sent two nights ago?'

Iori nodded. Although he was dressed in a light summer kimono and wooden slippers, he had swapped his bokken for a katana and a wakizashi, the shorter blade that Musashi favored for his two-sword fighting style.

'Whoever caused your father's delay is involved in a political plot aimed at creating unrest between the local daimyos and the Tokugawa shogunate,' I said. 'The principal instigator is someone who also wishes to take revenge for one of your father's previous foes. He must be aware of this.'

The Tokugawa shogunate was the ruling feudal military government of Japan. It was currently headed by Shogun Iemitsu Tokugawa, the third hereditary governor of the Tokugawa dynasty, the clan who came to power at the turn of the century.

Iori glanced at me, shadows leaping across his face from the flames of a nearby torch; we were making our way across the crowded bridge where I had stood when I first arrived in Osaka.

'Yes, he is. The ringleader is a member of a branch of the Yoshioka family, whom Father defeated some years ago.' Lines creased the young man's brow. 'The daimyos of Kansai are descended from families who have served the Tokugawa clan for centuries. On that front, there is no need to fear an uprising.' He paused. 'You do not have to look so surprised. I plan to become a vassal of one of the local lords myself. As such, I need to know the political landscape of my country.'

'I would be very pleased if you lived to see that day, Iori-kun,' I said in clipped tones.

We had reached a quiet backstreet some fifty feet from the riverbank. The noise of the main crowd was a dull roar to our right.

Iori stopped and looked around the deserted passage. 'This is the place.'

I frowned as I observed the area. 'The place for what?'

'The ambush,' replied Iori. He shrugged at my expression. 'Oh come now, there is only five of them. Besides, my father will not be long. He picked this spot himself.'

I stared at him, aghast. 'Who said anything about five men?'

Iori's eyes narrowed. 'You did.'

'I said fifteen!'

Tense silence descended between us. The shuffle of approaching footsteps reached my ears above the clamor coming from the direction of the river. Shadows shifted at either end of the alley.

'You wrote five in the letter,' said Iori between gritted teeth. He unsheathed his katana and wakizashi.

'I did?'

I stood with my back against his, eyes focused on the men closing in on us. My hands hung loosely at my sides. I left the blades at my waist untouched.

'Yes!' snapped Iori.

'Oh,' I said, chagrined.

We found ourselves inside a circle of gleaming blades and grim faces just as bangs erupted across the city. The brightly-colored sparks of fireworks painted the sky over the river in graceful arcs.

'It looks like you decided to stick around, *nanbanjin*,' said the leader of the mercenaries. He studied me with a cold, calculating look, his grip light on his katana and tanto dagger. 'I must admit to being curious as to your association with the Miyamotos. I would very much like to know the reason why you have been hanging around them before we kill you.'

'I want to become an apprentice to Miyamoto-dono,' I said lightly.

The man grinned. 'You wish to improve your fighting skills?'

I shrugged. 'Yes. There are some very bad men after me.'

The mercenary glanced at his companions, a shrewd smile curving his lips. 'We always need more warriors,' he drawled. 'Why not join us? I would be honored to teach you myself if you lay down your swords and walk away.'

Iori stiffened at my back.

'No, thank you,' I said. 'Besides, I hardly think a dead man could teach me anything.'

The mercenary's smile slipped from his face. 'You arrogant mongrel! You will—'

It was as far as he got. I whipped two loaded flintlock pistols from inside my vest, shot him in the chest, and fired at the man standing next to him. The reports were drowned by the cracks and booms from the fireworks display.

The thuds of the men's bodies falling to the ground

broke the frozen moment of stillness. Chaos erupted around us.

Knowing I would not have time to reload the pistols, I grabbed their handles and cast them like shurikens, the concealed short-bladed weapons I had seen Musashi throw during our duels. The guns whistled through the air and struck two men in the head. They stumbled, eyes rolling backward into their sockets. I drew my katana and wakizashi from my waist before they hit the dirt.

'How are you doing, Iori?' I shouted over my shoulder.

'Just shut up and fight!' snarled the young man. He wielded his swords expertly at the men facing him, his skills belying his age.

I grinned and engaged the figures charging toward me.

The mercenaries attacked with a ferocity born of desperation. With their leader dead and his second-in-command incapacitated by the shot to his abdomen, they had to capture the boy at all costs if they wanted to have a chance at negotiating with Musashi and the Osaka daimyo.

By the time we had disposed of half of them, Iori and I had sustained several cuts and were starting to tire.

'I will hold them here!' I said between pants, stabbing at one of our attackers. 'Leave!'

Iori glanced at me as he dropped below a deadly thrust, blood dripping from lacerations on his left arm and above his right eyebrow. 'Are you mad?'

'Trust me! There is more to me than meets the eye. I *will* survive this!'

Iori blocked a strike to his chest with his wakizashi. His eyes widened. 'That will not be necessary.'

I followed his gaze. My heart stuttered.

Musashi moved through the mercenaries like a ghost, the edges of his swords gleaming with crimson drops under the dazzling flares of the fireworks display. Men fell without knowing where the blow that killed them came from, their shocked expressions almost comical in death.

I watched, my breath frozen in my throat, enthralled by the spectacle of Musashi's dancing blades as he whirled across the passage, his swords moving in lightning fast thrusts and slashes.

There was no doubt in my mind that I would never again witness such perfect communion between a master and his weapons. For Musashi fought with a speed and grace that spoke of his complete command of the blades he wielded, as well as an absolute grasp of his enemy and the battlefield around him.

It seemed only seconds passed before we found ourselves standing in the midst of a whole lot of dead and disabled mercenaries. Rapturous applause exploded from the crowds gathered on the riverbank as the fireworks display reached its climax.

'That is the end of that,' said Musashi calmly. He stooped to wipe his blades on the clothes of one of the fallen men and glanced at the lights in the sky. 'Pity we missed the end of the festival.'

I stared at him, speechless for once.

'What happened at the castle?' I said finally, slowly sheathing my own swords.

'The daimyo's men arrested the samurai who had delayed me,' said Musashi. 'He is being questioned as we speak.'

I looked from Musashi to Iori and back, feeling

somewhat betrayed. 'So the lord knew what was going on?'

Musashi's brow creased. 'Of course. I could not very well hide such a conspiracy from the man whose roof I was staying under.'

'But you let him come out on his own!' I said, pointing at Iori.

The younger man grimaced. 'That is because we knew you would be there. Whether you are aware of it or not, your skills have improved with every duel you have fought with Father. The two of us could have handled five men until he got here.' He looked around. 'Of course, we were not to know from your appallingly composed message that there were going to be fifteen of them.'

'Ah.' I scratched my head. 'Yes, er, sorry about that.'

Guards appeared at one end of the alley. They rushed toward us, their swords drawn.

'It is quite all right,' Musashi called out. 'We have disposed of them.'

The guards slowed, their jaws sagging as they gazed at the figures littering the passage. They began disarming the wounded mercenaries.

'What now?' I muttered.

Musashi looked me up and down with a critical eye. 'Well, I guess we shall have to make you more presentable before we introduce you to the daimyo.'

'Huh?' My puzzled gaze swung between Musashi and Iori. 'What do you mean?'

'I cannot very well take you into the presence of the lord in the state that you are in,' said Musashi. 'It would be a disgrace for me as your master.'

My mouth went dry as his meaning sank in. 'You mean…you are taking me on as your apprentice?'

Musashi shrugged. 'It is either that or kill you. You are starting to unnerve the guards at the castle.' A faint smile crossed the samurai's lips. 'Besides, Iori agrees with me on this matter. Despite your barbaric way of fighting, we believe you show enough promise to be considered a worthy apprentice.'

I looked at the young man. Iori avoided my gaze.

'You are still a crazy *nanbanjin* though,' he mumbled, shuffling his feet. 'And do not think I will go easy on you. You shall be a junior apprentice, so you will have to answer to me, your senior.'

I grinned. 'I look forward to it.'

Musashi's smile slowly faded. The great man sighed. 'Before we get to that though, we seriously need to do something about that disgraceful chicken scribbling you call handwriting.'

THE END

THE MEETING

A SEVENTEEN SERIES SHORT STORY

A.D. STARRLING

THE COLT MUSTANG POCKETLITE IS ONE OF THE SMALLEST and most consistently reliable concealed-carry firearms on the US market today. A scaled down version of the original Colt M1911, a recoil-operated, semi-automatic, single-action pistol popular among the US Armed Forces and law-enforcement agencies alike, the Pocketlite is 5.5 inches long, weighs just under thirteen ounces, and has a 6+1 round capacity.

These facts ran through Reid Hasley's mind as he stared into the stainless steel barrel of one such gun. Particularly the part about the round capacity.

How the hell did we end up in this situation?

'You don't want to do this, Dennis,' he said in a steady voice.

Detective Chris Lockett, his partner in the Boston PD Homicide Unit, shifted slightly a couple of feet to his right.

Reid kept his gaze focused on the pale, sweaty young man who stood on the other side of the front room of the shabby, second-floor apartment in South Boston.

Dennis Wittman was a key witness to a violent armed robbery, assault, and attempted homicide perpetrated by two masked men the previous night at a 7-11 franchise on Broadway. It had taken Reid and Lockett three hours of going through CCTV recordings to finally identify him as the skinny male who had been standing on the corner of the road when the suspects ran out of the store. One of the men stumbled into Wittman and pushed him to the ground before fleeing into the night. As such, Wittman was one of two people who had gotten close enough to the suspects to be able to help with their identification. The other was Fernando Lopez, the 7-11 night store manager currently fighting for his life in the intensive care unit at the Massachusetts General Hospital.

Wittman was known to the police for a previous DUI and two counts of possession of a Class D substance. According to his probation officer, he was now clean and ready to embrace a life free of crime. Which didn't quite explain the presence of the gun currently clasped in his damp, shaking hand.

They hadn't seen a license for a firearm in his records. And they certainly hadn't expected to be faced with one when they came upon the open door of his rental apartment sixty seconds ago and entered the place to clear it.

'Look, we just want to talk to you about what happened last night,' said Lockett.

Reid avoided looking at his partner. A seasoned patrol officer and a sergeant, Lockett only made detective eight months ago. Although the man was an experienced cop, Reid knew this was Lockett's first time looking at the wrong end of a gun. As a Marine turned homicide detective, Reid was a seasoned veteran who had seen plenty of firefights and knew how to handle them.

Right now, Lockett's body language reminded him of some of the young soldiers who saw action for the first time on the battlefield. The jumpy ones who got themselves and their friends killed.

He consciously dropped his shoulders and adopted a relaxed posture. 'You were outside the 7-11 on Broadway last night when those robbers ran out. We saw you on a CCTV recording.'

Wittman twitched. Reid's gaze flicked to the wavering gun in his hand before returning to the man's ashen face and dilated pupils. He could read more than fear in Wittman's eyes. The guy was high on something.

'The man those robbers shot is in a critical condition in hospital. We just want to talk to you about what you saw.' Reid paused. 'You'll be helping us out, Dennis. Just put the gun down and we can—'

'Na-huh!' Wittman's voice quavered almost as badly as his hand. 'I had nothing to do with that shit! You—you guys are just trying to con me! I'm not going back to jail, you hear?'

He jutted his chin out and tightened his grip on the gun.

Reid bit back a sigh. *Great. Drug-induced paranoia. That's all we need right now.*

A balmy breeze blew through the open window to the left and rattled the metal blinds. Sweat prickled Reid's scalp.

It was the height of summer and Boston was in the grip of one of the worst heat waves the city had seen in over a decade. The crime rate had risen proportionally, with assaults and homicides skyrocketing to levels seldom seen before.

Reid allowed a small smile to cross his lips. 'No one is going to take you to jail, Dennis.' *Well, not straightaway, anyway.*

'I'm sure we can persuade the prosecutor's office to look leniently on your case,' Lockett added stiffly.

Wittman's eyes widened, panic radiating off him almost as badly as the stench of sweat.

Reid masked a wince. *Bad choice of words.*

At this rate, the breeze was going to be blowing through a hole in his or Lockett's stomach in the next minute or so. It was time for action. He took two steps forward.

Wittman startled. 'What—what are doing?'

Reid shrugged. 'I'm going to take that gun off you.'

Lockett drew a breath in sharply behind him.

Wittman gaped. 'Are you crazy?'

'Well, no,' Reid drawled. 'You see, I can tell you haven't had that gun for long.'

'Huh?' Wittman blinked owlishly. 'How—how can you—?'

'The safety's still on.'

By the time Wittman looked down and realized he had just been told a lie, Reid was already moving. He leapt onto the coffee table, jumped just as Wittman's arm rose, and tackled the skinny man to the ground. They landed hard on the floor.

Wittman's finger flexed on the trigger. A bullet whistled past Reid's head and ricocheted off the metal lampshade in the ceiling. He knocked the gun out of Wittman's hand, saw the man's other fist coming toward his face, blocked the blow, and punched him. Blood spurted from Wittman's nose. His eyes rolled back in his skull and he went limp.

'Shit,' said Lockett.

Reid looked over his shoulder. His gaze dropped to where his partner stared; the bullet had smacked into the ground a couple of inches from the detective's left foot.

'You okay?' He took his cuffs out, rolled the unconscious Wittman onto his front, and closed them around the man's wrists.

'Er, yeah.' Lockett sounded dazed.

'You better call it in.'

Reid hauled Wittman up onto the couch, patted him down, and extracted two small bags of a white powder from the rear pocket of his jeans.

Lockett took his cell out, dialed Control, and requested a uniform patrol unit to transport Wittman to the local District C-6 station.

It was 14:00 by the time they finished processing Wittman's apartment. Apart from a couple of spare magazines for the Pocketlite and another stash of drugs taped to the back of a wardrobe, they found little of interest.

Reid stood on the hot asphalt outside the police station and glanced at the dazzling, golden sphere in the sky. Wittman had been charged with obstructing a law enforcement officer and assault by means of a dangerous weapon. It would be several hours before he was in a fit state to answer questions about the incident at the 7-11. The more time passed, the slimmer their chances of catching the perpetrators of the crime became. He sighed and climbed in the car with Lockett.

They were approaching Dorchester Street when the call came through on the radio.

'All units in the vicinity of Fox, please be advised that we have a Code 105 in progress on East 3rd St, near the corner with P St. Rapid Deployment Protocol is in effect. Responding officer requesting assistance.' The dispatcher gave the full address.

Lockett looked at Reid. 'It's the heat isn't it? It's gotta be the heat bringing all the crazies out.'

Reid switched the emergency light on and stepped on the gas.

Fox was the unit designation for the District C-6

station. Code 105 meant an active shooter situation. They were one mile from the location.

Lockett called dispatch just as they barreled across the junction onto East Broadway. 'Control, this is 2459. Please advise the Duty Supervisor in Homicide that we're responding to the request for assistance at the Code 105.'

'Copy, 2459.'

Their Duty Supervisor for the day was Lieutenant Reginald Brooks. Reid smiled grimly. An army veteran himself, Brooks would be pissed if they missed the action.

It took under two minutes to reach the junction of East 3rd and P St. Reid saw two cops crouching behind the open door of a patrol vehicle angled across the road some hundred and fifty feet ahead. He braked and spun the steering wheel around. The Ford Victoria screeched to a stop with the broadside facing the intersection. Sirens blared behind them as they stepped out of their vehicle; a patrol car was charging down East 3rd toward the junction.

Lockett signaled to the officers behind the windshield. The driver flashed his lights and turned north in a squeal of tires; he would go around and block off the other end of the road to establish a perimeter.

Reid and Lockett drew their guns and jogged along the north pavement toward the responding officers' vehicle. Curtains and blinds twitched behind windows on both sides of the road. Reid caught glimpses of pale, worried faces. This was a nice, working-class neighborhood, with tidy front gardens and well-kept houses; the residents had likely never seen anything on this scale before.

A shot rang out just as they reached the corner of a

drive. They ducked and ran across the road to the patrol car.

'Detective Sergeant Hasley, Detective Lockett, Homicide,' Reid said briskly as they dropped by the side of the cops squatting in the cover of the vehicle.

'Officer Johnson,' said the female officer. 'This is Officer Tolino.'

Reid acknowledged the somber man beside her with a nod.

'Can you brief us?' he asked Johnson.

The patrol car that had gone around the block screeched to a halt across the junction four hundred feet away, sirens muted and lights flashing.

'We responded to a domestic disturbance call twelve minutes ago,' said Johnson. 'On our way here, Control informed us that the neighbor who reported the incident called 911 again and said he'd heard screaming and two gunshots. We got here at 14:03. A man came out of the property and fired at our patrol car and the neighbor's garden before running back inside. He's fired two more shots out of the left front window since, including the one you just heard.'

Reid eyed the pretty, one-storey, blue clapboard house fifty feet northeast of where they crouched.

'We just heard from Control,' said Tolino. 'The property's owner was involved in a traffic accident last year, so they had some records. The house is registered to a Burt Suarez. Married. Works the tollbooth at the Tobin Bridge. Firearms Records Bureau shows a License to Carry for a Smith & Wesson 908. Description from motor vehicles registry matches the gunman.'

'Kids?' said Reid sharply.

'Not that records show,' said Johnson.

The officer looked as relieved as Reid felt. The last thing anyone wanted was children involved in an active shooter situation.

'He shot the neighbor's dog,' Tolino added with a grimace. 'Poor thing's still alive. Neighbor ran out and carried it inside the house two minutes ago. You can hear it whining if you listen hard enough.'

Lockett's grip tightened on his Glock. 'What kind of sick bastard shoots a dog?'

'One who isn't thinking straight,' Reid murmured, his gaze focused on the house. 'Is that his car out front?'

Johnson and Tolino glanced at the black Volvo parked at the curb.

Johnson frowned. 'No. His is the Toyota behind it. There are no other vehicles registered at the address.'

More sirens sounded from the west and south as other patrol units raced toward their location.

'Have you heard anyone scream or shout for help since you got here?' said Reid quietly.

'Negative,' Johnson replied. 'And 911 hasn't received any calls from this address either.'

Reid studied Johnson and narrowed his eyes. *We all know this doesn't look to be a hostage situation with a barricaded gunman. There are dead or injured people in that house. And God only knows how many spare magazines the guy has.*

'Broadcast our assessment of the situation to all responding units, tell them the safest approach, and get a secure perimeter established,' Reid said curtly.

Johnson reached inside the car and grabbed the radio handset.

Reid twisted on his heels and indicated their Ford Victoria at the crossroad. 'We can establish a temporary command post there until S.W.A.T. arrives—'

'Oh fuck,' Lockett whispered.

Reid whipped his head around and followed his partner's frozen gaze. His mouth went dry.

A girl in her late teens had come out of a house one hundred feet up the road. She had headphones on and was leading a small white terrier on a leash. She turned and headed along the north side pavement toward them, eyes cast down and head bobbing along to whatever music she was listening to.

She was fifty feet from the front porch of the gunman's house.

Johnson swore and jumped to her feet. 'Hey! Hey, you there! *Stop!*' She waved her arm frantically above her head.

Reid caught motion at the window of the gunman's house. 'Get down!'

He yanked Johnson by her belt. She gasped and dropped back to his side.

The terrier started barking. The girl gave him a puzzled glance, picked him up, and carried on walking down the road. The dog squirmed in her arms.

They were now twenty feet from the gunman's porch.

Reid felt his pulse accelerate. With S.W.A.T. not yet on site, they would have to move in to save the girl.

'Lockett, you and I are point. Johnson, you're rear guard. Tolino, tell Control and responding units we're moving in to rescue a potential victim, then cover us.' He glanced at the tense faces around him. 'Just remember your training. On the count of three.'

Reid inched to the edge of the bumper, gripped his Glock in both hands, and started the countdown. 'One.'

Lockett and Johnson moved into position next to him. Tolino grabbed the radio and started talking in a low, urgent voice to dispatch.

'Two.'

The gunman's front door opened. Suarez stepped out and raised his gun at the girl.

'*Three!*'

Reid shot up and sprinted toward the property, arms straight out and finger moving on the trigger of the Glock. His first shot went wild. His second smacked into a wooden post next to Suarez's head. The man whirled around and jumped back into the cover of the doorway.

The girl stopped. Her head snapped up. Her eyes widened.

'*Get down!*' Reid yelled.

She stood frozen, color draining from her face.

'For God's sake, drop to the ground!' Lockett shouted.

The girl cried out and crumpled to the pavement, the barking terrier clasped tightly within the cover of her body. Her broken sobs were drowned out by the sound of gunfire from the house.

Reid cursed and angled toward a rhododendron bush to the left. There was a gasp behind him. He looked over his shoulder.

A bullet had found Lockett's right arm. The detective dropped down by a picket fence and gripped his limb.

Acid burned Reid's throat when Johnson cried out and stumbled. She clasped the bleeding gunshot wound to her outer thigh and fell to one knee.

He scowled and shot repeatedly at the dim figure in

the doorway of the house. *Either this guy has some serious beginner's luck or he's a regular on a firing range!*

Johnson's shout made him look around.

'No! Get back!'

She waved violently to where Tolino hovered by the bumper of the patrol car, struggled to her feet, and hobbled to where Lockett squatted by the fence.

Reid opened his mouth to shout the same command just as three shots shattered the muggy afternoon.

The only reason Tolino didn't die that day was because it was that much harder to hit a moving target. The first two bullets struck the front wing of the car as he dove for cover. The third one went straight through his left shoulder.

The girl with the terrier screamed, scrambled to her knees, and crawled hastily backward the way she had come, the dog struggling in her grasp. She was under cover a moment later.

Lockett darted out into the road and pulled Tolino to the safety of the fence. Suarez disappeared from view and slammed the front door shut.

A distant crash came from the rear of the property seconds later.

Reid moved swiftly toward the house and caught a glimpse of Suarez as he legged it across his backyard. He turned and eyed the three wounded officers behind him, his heart pounding in his chest.

'Go get him!' snapped Lockett.

'We're fine!' said Johnson. Tolino bobbed his head jerkily next to her.

Reid twisted on his heels, vaulted over the picket fence

fronting the property, and sprinted in the direction where Suarez had disappeared.

He stopped near the backend of the building, changed the magazine in his Glock, and stole a look around the corner.

Suarez was climbing over a wooden fence at the bottom of his garden.

Reid rounded the building and bolted across the grass. He reached the palisade within seconds, jumped up against it, and grabbed the top with both hands. He peeked carefully over. An empty plot of land lay on the other side. Suarez was already halfway across it.

Reid scaled the fence and went after him. He emerged onto a road and saw the gunman vanish over a cinder block wall ahead and to the left. He bit back a curse.

The guy was headed for the water.

Two patrol cars squealed into view some five hundred feet to the left. Reid signaled them to go north and dashed across the street. His breaths came hard and fast as he climbed the brick wall. He found himself facing the deserted parking lot of an abandoned warehouse. Suarez was a rapidly disappearing figure on the cracked, overgrown asphalt.

Christ! For a large man, the guy sure knows how to run.

Sweat was pouring freely down the back of Reid's neck by the time he exited the lot. Suarez had crossed yet another road and was climbing a chain-link fence overlooking a wide expanse of derelict land.

The noise of rotors punctuated the rising cacophony of sirens as he chased after the running gunman. He caught the flash of lights out the corner of his eyes and glimpsed the small, blue and gray body of a Massachusetts

State Police helicopter in the sky to the north just as he reached the chain-link. Reid clambered rapidly over the barrier and dropped down hard on a strip of chipped asphalt. The shock of the landing jarred his knees. He gritted his teeth and took off after Suarez.

The gunman was running toward the shimmering green waters of a channel some thousand feet ahead. The piers and terminals of the Port of Boston rose beyond it, with the harbor to the east.

Reid cursed. The last thing he wanted to do was go for a swim if Suarez decided to jump. He had to stop the man before he reached the water.

He raced past rust-covered shipping containers and dilapidated metal sheds. Asphalt gave way to dirt. Four hundred feet later, the outlook opened out onto overgrown grass and scrubland. A flicker of hope darted through him.

Suarez's speed had dropped. He was now some two hundred feet away and running toward an abandoned dock out on the water.

Reid scanned the structure as he pounded the ground after the gunman.

A crane sat atop a metal tower to the right of the platform. To the left stood an abandoned cabin. Walkways connected the dock to the mainland and two small landings on either side.

Suarez reached the closest gangway thirteen seconds ahead of him. He stumbled over some uneven boards, faltered for a moment, and kept on going. Sweat formed a growing dark patch on the back of his shirt.

Wooden planks juddered beneath Reid's feet as he bolted onto the walkway.

Suarez stopped twenty feet shy of the dock, whirled around, and fired in his direction. Reid didn't even flinch. The shot went wild. Suarez turned and dashed toward the platform.

Movement to the left caught Reid's gaze. He slowed a fraction, his stomach plummeting. *You gotta be kidding me!*

The cabin had obscured the far left side of the dock from the mainland. Now that he'd gotten closer, the area beyond it was visible.

A figure was rising from the corner of the platform. A man. He teetered slightly and righted himself inches from the water's edge. Sunlight glinted on the beer bottle in his hand and the half dozen empty ones littering the ground by his feet.

Reid groaned. *A drunk. That's all I goddamn need!*

Suarez had reached the tower. He ran past it and staggered to an almost comical stop when he spotted the man who stood facing him across the dock.

The drunk said something and offered his bottle to Suarez, a friendly if inebriated smile dawning on his face.

Reid's jaw sagged. *That moron!*

He opened his mouth to shout a warning to the intoxicated man.

Suarez took three steps toward the stranger, raised his gun, and shot him point-blank in the head.

The bullet entered the man's skull just above the bridge of his nose. It exited the back of his head a microsecond later in a small spray of blood. He fell to his knees and thudded side down onto the dock.

Anger squeezed Reid's heart. There would be no reasoning with Burt Suarez.

The gunman twisted on his heels and backed across

the dock past the dead man, his face a pale, blank mask as he swung his gun around and fired toward the walkway.

Reid bolted onto the platform and dove behind the tower, blood pounding in his ears. Bullets pinged off the metal framework and whizzed through the gaps between the steel struts. He moved into the cover of one of the posts.

Black-clad S.W.A.T. officers appeared in the gaps between the shipping containers on the other side of the deserted strip. The helicopter was a growing shape in the sky to the right.

Fifty feet ahead of him, Suarez reloaded his Smith & Wesson and raised the gun once more. A noise stopped him in his tracks. Small and innocuous, it was staggeringly shocking under the circumstances.

Although he didn't know it at the time, that noise would forever alter the path of Reid's life and challenge everything he had come to accept as reality.

The sound was that of a man groaning.

Suarez's head moved mechanically as he looked to his left.

The dead man blinked and released the beer bottle in his hand.

It rolled across the deck and came to a stop by the gunman's feet, spilling some of its contents across his left shoe.

The dead man sat up slowly. Blue eyes narrowed beneath the trickle of blood marking his skin. He touched the hole in his forehead gingerly.

'That hurt,' he said accusingly to Suarez. He climbed unsteadily to his feet.

Suarez gaped, took a step back, and swung the Smith and Wesson at the dead man once more.

Reid walked out of the cover of the tower with his Glock raised and pulled the trigger twice.

The bullets struck Suarez in the chest. He jerked back with a short cry and fell heavily on the platform. The Smith & Wesson clattered out of his hand and pinwheeled across the dock. It hit the dead man's right foot.

He glanced from the weapon to the red stains blooming across Suarez's chest, looked over to Reid, carefully raised his hands in the air, and kicked the gun toward him.

'Hey there,' he said in a slightly embarrassed voice.

Reid stared, unsure how to respond.

'I could have sworn you died,' he said finally.

The man hesitated. 'What, from this?' He indicated the wound in his forehead. 'It's just a scratch.'

'I saw the bullet exit the back of your skull,' Reid countered dully.

The man blinked.

'What bullet?' he said innocently.

Reid looked past him. The shell was nowhere to be seen. *Shit. It must have hit the water.*

He narrowed his eyes. 'Your chest wasn't moving for a good while there, pal.'

The man shrugged. 'I'm a shallow breather.'

It was at that point that the cavalry arrived.

A SHADOW FELL ACROSS THE DESK. REID LOOKED UP INTO

the stern face of Lieutenant Reginald Brooks, his direct superior in the Homicide Unit.

The man placed a steaming cup of coffee in front of him. 'How're you doing?'

Reid thanked him for the drink. 'Fine.'

Brooks furrowed his heavily-lined brow. 'You know this investigation is just routine, right? Your service records from the military are spotless. This is the first time you've discharged your weapon since you joined the force and it was an active shooter situation at that. The whole thing was resolved pretty damn quickly, considering.'

Reid sighed. Two days had passed since the deadly events in South Boston.

On the day of his untimely death, Burt Suarez had been relieved from an early shift at the toll bridge by one of his colleagues. He came home to surprise his wife, spotted his brother's car parked outside, and walked in to find them in bed together. Suarez had reportedly been a devoted Christian who cherished his spouse above all else. He was said to have been kind to man and animal alike.

As in almost every case of homicide, love and hate were the primary emotions involved on that hot summer's day. Burt Suarez lost his senses when he witnessed this ultimate betrayal, leading him to commit the violent acts that took the lives of his wife and brother, and wounded three police officers.

In the aftermath of what happened, Reid was placed on administrative leave, as per standard practice. Whenever a police officer used his gun in the line of duty, irrespective of intent, circumstances, and whether the action resulted in someone's injury or death, the department's Internal Affairs had to carry out an investigation into the incident. He would have to wait for their final decision and that of the department's psychiatrist before he could resume active duty. With Lockett out of action for at least another week, he'd spent his time writing reports and had started to work his way through the backlog of paperwork sitting in his in-tray.

Brooks patted him on the shoulder. 'It'll fly by. You'll be back on the streets in no time.' He turned and headed toward his office.

Reid watched him leave, grateful for the talk. The support his colleagues and fellow officers had shown him in the last forty-eight hours, including their Superintendent, had also been welcome. Still, it sucked to be stuck behind a desk.

His gaze landed on a file next to the computer. The papers inside had started to curl at the edges from the number of times he'd read it. It contained a copy of the statement from the drunk Suarez had shot at the dock, as well as a detailed background investigation he himself had carried out on the man.

His name was Lucas Soul. Born in Brooklyn in 1966, he moved to Boston at age twenty-four, after completing a degree from the John Jay College of Criminal Justice and gaining investigative experience with a PI firm in New York. He now owned his own detective agency in Bay Village. He had no known next of kin, was single with no dependents, and had no criminal records.

Reid frowned. *The guy is just too...neat.*

He hesitated before flicking the folder open. Soul's face stared back at him from a copy of his driver's license, his gaze as inscrutable as it had been that day on the dock. Reid leaned back in his chair and linked his hands behind his head.

There was no denying what he had seen that day on the dock. Although they hadn't recovered the missing slug, and despite the medical report stating the guy had suffered a non-life-threatening head injury, Reid knew Lucas Soul should be six feet under right now.

The fact that he wasn't weighed heavily on Reid's mind. It was all he'd been able to think about in the last forty-eight hours, something that didn't escape his estranged wife when he visited her and their two children yesterday, at the house they used to share in the suburbs of Boston. Although their relationship had cooled somewhat in the last three years, he still got along with Samantha and she knew him well enough to know when something was troubling him.

Reid frowned. He didn't believe in miracles, medical or otherwise, not when he'd seen Soul die as clearly as he had. He drummed his fingers on the table and glanced at his in-tray.

The paperwork could wait.

He took his own car and headed across town to Bay Village.

Poseidon Security was located in a quiet side street with antique gas lamps. He parked around the corner from the address and strolled along the sun-dappled pavement to a pretty, red-brick Victorian building. A flight of steps led to a communal front door. The nameplates on the wall next to it indicated that Poseidon Security was on the second floor. There were three other offices in the building; an accountant, a financial advisor, and an architect. He pressed the buzzer for the PI agency.

Twenty seconds passed. The intercom remained silent.

Reid pushed the button again.

The door opened. A beautiful blonde with long hair in a ponytail and close-fitting gym wear stepped out with a sports bike.

'Oh.' She stopped and blinked at him.

Reid smiled. 'The architect?'

Her cheeks dimpled, lips parting to reveal a dazzling smile. 'The accountant, actually. Who are you here to see?'

'Poseidon Security.'

The woman's eyes brightened and a slight flush stained her cheekbones. 'I haven't seen Lucas yet this morning. He shouldn't be too long. Do you want to wait outside his office?'

'Sure.'

Reid paused in the doorway and watched the blonde get on the bike. She cycled down the road, golden hair fluttering in the breeze. He spotted at least three men who turned and stared at her.

Soul is a lucky bastard.

He turned, entered the lobby, and headed up carpeted stairs to the second floor.

He'd asked several detectives in the Downtown and Charlestown stations about Soul earlier that morning. A couple of them had come across the private investigator in the past and reported he was an efficient and level-headed guy. Which made Reid all the more curious about the man.

Why had he been flat-out drunk and alone on that dock?

There was more to Lucas Soul than met the eye.

He found the office at the end of a corridor. The frosted glass in the top half of the door boasted the name of the PI firm in simple yet elegant writing. A pair of chairs framed a small side table with a stack of magazines next to it. Reid took a seat and picked the top one. It was last month's copy of *The Economist.*

An hour and several mind-numbingly boring business articles later, Reid sighed and rose to his feet. Soul had obviously decided to have a protracted lie-in. Either that or he was on a dock somewhere, getting drunk.

A phone rang on the floor above. The low hubbub of conversation rose from the office at the other end of the hall.

Reid removed his wallet from his jacket, slipped a small lock pick set out, and went to work on the door of Poseidon Security. He was inside in less than a minute.

The office was large and brightly lit. Two desks were set at a slight angle next to the tall windows overlooking the sunny street outside. Both had slick computers sitting atop them and ergonomic chairs. Filing cabinets and bookcases lined the wall to the left. Facing them across the way was an eclectic collection of different-sized canvas paintings in gold-colored frames.

Two internal doors opened off the space. One led to a bathroom and a fire exit, the other a comfortable sitting room with a pull-out sofa bed and a kitchenette. Reid strolled back to the main area and studied the desks.

The one to the right looked vacant.

He turned and took the seat behind the left desk. A pair of full metal trays sat next to the computer. He flicked through the paperwork. Most of it comprised requests for surveillance work for attorneys and employee checks for investment banks. Reid cocked an eyebrow at the names of the companies. No wonder Soul could afford an office in Bay Village.

He started to go through the drawers. A voice made him freeze ten seconds later.

'You know, this is technically breaking and entering.'

Reid looked up slowly.

Soul was leaning in the open doorway of his office. He was dressed in jeans and a T-shirt and was holding a paper coffee cup in his hand. There was a small dressing on his forehead.

Reid narrowed his eyes. He hadn't heard the guy come in. 'What are you, a cat?'

Soul's lips twitched. 'I bumped into Jennifer on the way here.'

'Jennifer?' Reid pushed back from the desk and rose to his feet. 'Is that the accountant?'

'Uh-huh.'

Reid rubbed the back of his head, feeling awkward at being caught in the act. His hand stilled. 'Hang on a minute. That was an hour ago!'

Soul gazed at him blankly. 'I know. I stayed out for lunch.'

Reid scowled. 'You mean you *deliberately* made me wait?'

Soul shrugged, walked in, and closed the door.

'You trying to avoid me or something?' Reid said in a belligerent tone.

Soul raised an eyebrow. 'Can you blame me?'

Reid hesitated. The guy wasn't exactly in the wrong.

Soul took a sip of his coffee. 'So, what can I do for you, Detective Hasley?'

Reid stared, nonplussed, at the man facing him across the room.

Why am I here, exactly? What the hell was I hoping to achieve by turning up at this guy's place, uninvited, and going through his stuff?

Soul waited silently for his reply, his posture relaxed.

Reid glanced at the empty desk. 'Do you have a partner?'

Something shifted in Soul's eyes then.

'I did,' he replied quietly.

The words that left Reid's mouth next astounded him as much as they seemed to surprise Soul. 'You looking for a replacement?'

Soul drew a breath in sharply. His eyes darkened.

Though shock still reverberated through him, Reid detected a flash of pain and anger in the blue depths.

Soul recovered his composure and adopted a nonchalant air. 'You propositioning me, officer?'

Reid grimaced. 'Sorry, you're not my type.'

Soul's lips twitched again.

'So, will you think about it?' said Reid.

Soul sobered. 'Are you serious?'

Reid's heart thudded against his ribs. He still had no idea why he'd said what he'd just said. He hadn't realized he'd started to grow weary of the homicide unit until he'd seen the empty desk in Soul's office.

There was also the mystery of how Soul had survived that bullet. That was what had drawn Reid to come and meet the man again. Lucas Soul was an anomaly in this world. Although his records showed his life to be a straightforward existence, Reid sensed it was too good to be true. It was as if he had reinvented himself to hide his true nature.

Reid was convinced the reality would be beyond anything he had ever experienced. Fate had placed Soul in his path for a reason. He was determined to find out why.

Soul sighed.

'What?' said Reid.

'I don't like that look on your face.'

Reid blinked. 'Why?'

'I sense you're about to become a pain in my ass.'

THE APARTMENT BLOCK WAS LOCATED IN FENWAY, LESS than half a mile from the home of the Boston Red Sox. Reid stood across the street from the building and studied its upper levels. Two were completely dark. Lights were on behind the windows of a single apartment on the tenth floor.

Four weeks had passed since the fatal shootout in South Boston. Internal Affairs had cleared Reid of any wrongdoing and he had returned to active duty over a fortnight ago, following a positive report from the psychiatrist.

Though he was happy to be back on the job, Reid had been unable to shake his single-minded wish to become Soul's business partner. He had spoken to Brooks and Lockett briefly about his intentions to leave Boston PD and had looked into the necessary certification procedure to become a private detective in the State of Massachusetts.

There was only one problem. Convincing Soul to

agree to his proposal had proven impossible so far. Reid wasn't sure why the man was so adamant he didn't need a partner when it was clear from the paperwork he'd seen at the office that he did.

Something told him it had to do with Soul's presence on that dock.

In the last four weeks, he had visited the PI at his office and various other places where he hung out. The last time had been four days ago, when he walked into the guy's favorite Italian restaurant in South End.

Soul looked up from his beer when Reid slid into the booth seat opposite him. He narrowed his eyes. 'You're turning into a stalker.'

Reid shrugged and took a menu from the holder next to the napkin stand. A waitress came to the table with a carafe of water and slipped her order pad out of the front pocket of her uniform.

'I've have the usual please,' said Soul.

'Classic pizza, hold the pepperoni, and a side salad?' said the waitress with a smile.

Soul nodded.

Reid stared. 'What's your problem with pepperoni?'

Soul gave him a cold look. The waitress eyed Reid questioningly.

'I'll have your Meat Lovers pizza and a beer. No salad.'

The restaurant was busy and the hubbub of conversation washed over them after the waitress left. They looked silently at each other.

'The answer's still no,' said Soul.

Reid frowned. 'I've seen your caseload. You need a partner.'

Soul leaned back in his seat and crossed his arms. 'I'll manage.'

Reid raised an eyebrow. 'You'll lose clients.'

Soul did not respond to the bait.

Reid looked around the restaurant. 'This is a nice place.'

Soul remained mute.

'So was that Chinese last week and the Mexican the week before that,' said Reid. 'That coffee place wasn't too shabby either.'

Soul grunted. 'You're picking up the tab for this one.'

They'd spent the rest of the evening talking sports, politics, and world affairs, like they had on the previous occasions Reid had shadowed Soul. By the end of the night, the PI's decision about a possible partnership remained unchanged.

That had been Friday just gone. Reid continued to stare at the building across the street, a half-smile playing on his lips. Was he pushing his luck coming here?

He crossed the road presently and entered the lobby of the apartment block. He took the lift to the tenth floor and strolled down a carpeted corridor to a door in the middle of the passage. There was a call box next to it. He pressed the buzzer.

A voice came through the intercom seconds later. 'Yes?'

'It's me,' said Reid.

Silence travelled through the speaker. It was followed by a loud sigh.

Locks turned on the inside of the door a moment later. Soul opened it with a tumbler in hand and subjected him to an exasperated stare. He was barefoot and dressed in dark sweatpants and a T-shirt.

'This is unusual and cruel punishment,' he said sullenly.

'I don't know what you're talking about.' Reid walked past him and entered the apartment. 'I'm just a friend visiting another friend.'

'Come on in,' said Soul sarcastically. 'And last I checked, we weren't friends.'

'That's cold, man.'

Reid headed down a hallway to a large, elegantly furnished living room. A fireplace dominated the wall to the right. A beautiful painting took pride of place above the mantelpiece.

'Nice.'

Reid sat down in a leather chair. He glanced from Soul to the bottle of whisky on the coffee table.

Soul rolled his eyes, walked over to a drinks cabinet, and returned with a tumbler full of ice. He poured in a generous amount of whisky, handed it to Reid, and topped his own glass.

'Thanks.'

Reid took a sip of the whisky and watched Soul sit on the couch. He paused and stared into the glass. 'This is nice.'

'It should be,' Soul muttered. 'It's a fifty-year-old Macallan.'

The TV in the corner of the room was on mute. It was showing a rerun of *It's a Wonderful Life*.

'Mind if I smoke?'

'Yes, I do, actually,' said Soul.

Reid paused, the packet of Pall Mall already halfway out of his jacket pocket.

He slipped it back inside and frowned faintly. 'This could be a deal breaker.'

Soul looked toward the heavens. 'Oh please, let it be.'

A comfortable silence fell across the room.

'So, is the answer still no?' said Reid.

Soul sighed. 'Has anyone told you you're a stubborn bastard?'

'Yes. My soon-to-be-ex-wife.'

Soul's gaze flicked to the wedding ring on Reid's finger. 'You got kids?'

'Two,' said Reid. He took another sip of the whisky and allowed himself a small smile. 'Sophie is five going on fifteen. Spencer is three.'

The expression that flashed through Soul's eyes made him pause. Though brief, what he glimpsed spoke of infinite loneliness and yearning on a scale he had never before seen.

'How old are you?' he said.

Soul stiffened slightly.

'You've seen my file,' he said in a level voice.

Reid studied him for silent seconds. 'I don't believe you're thirty-four.'

'And why is that?'

Reid hesitated.

'Your eyes,' he said quietly. 'They're...older than your years.'

Soul stared at him, his face unreadable once more.

Reid felt the hair rise on the back of his neck. His instincts told him he was on the right track. 'You look like someone who's lived through a lifetime of experiences, most of them painful.'

Soul broke contact with his intent gaze and looked down into his glass.

Reid thought back to everything he had seen and knew about the man. There was something else, something he only registered at that very moment. The eerie feeling gripping him intensified.

'Your head,' he muttered.

'What about it?'

'Your wound. It's gone.' Reid stared at the unblemished skin above Soul's eyes. 'There's no scar.'

Soul downed his glass and refilled it.

Reid gazed at the man on the couch, his pulse thrumming rapidly in his ears. Curiosity won out over apprehension.

'What are you?'

Soul dropped his head back on the couch and stared at the ceiling.

A wild thought ran through Reid's mind. He tensed. 'You're not a werewolf, are you?'

Soul looked at him then. 'What would you do if I was?'

Reid scratched his cheek. 'Well, I'd make sure I always carried a silver bullet and a stake with me, just in case you went on a rampage.'

Lines furrowed Soul's smooth brow. 'Okay, I get the silver bullet, but why the stake?'

'Backup.'

Soul laughed.

Reid grinned and relaxed in the chair. 'You're warming to me.'

'You really are a stubborn son of a bitch, aren't you?'

'Yes, I am.' Reid paused. 'So, is that a yes?'

Soul shook his head and muttered something under his breath. 'Will you give up if I say no?'

'No,' Reid said bluntly. 'We'll be having pizza every Friday night until you agree to my demand. Chinese and Mexican give me acid, so you're safe there.'

Soul sighed and ran a hand through his hair.

'So, what are you?' Reid said.

Soul grimaced. 'That's a rather personal question.'

Reid stared. 'Okay. Why were you drunk that day at the dock?'

Soul narrowed his eyes. 'Another personal question.'

'Sheesh,' Reid muttered. He rubbed his chin thoughtfully. 'What about the accountant? You got a thing going on with her?'

Soul looked genuinely surprised for the first time that evening. 'Who, Jennifer?'

Reid sighed. 'No, the Hunchback of Notre-Dame. Of course, Jennifer. She's gorgeous and she's got the hots for you.'

Soul raised an eyebrow. 'She does?'

Reid frowned. 'You're kidding me, right?'

Soul hesitated. 'I don't…do relationships.'

Reid snorted. 'What are you, a monk?'

'No!' Soul rocked the glass from side to side and watched the movement of the amber liquid inside. 'Let's just say bad things happen to the people who hang around me.'

Reid registered the indirect warning. 'I'm a big boy. I know how to look after myself.'

Soul studied him for a while. He took another gulp of his whisky, put the glass down on the table, and leaned forward with his elbows on his thighs. He stared at the floor between his feet.

'Three months,' he said brusquely.

Reid blinked.

Soul looked up. 'I'll give you a three-month trial. You'll have to quit the Homicide Unit.'

'Not a problem. And make it six months.'

Soul frowned. 'Four.'

'Five,' Reid countered. 'And we'll change the name of the agency. I don't like fish.'

'Poseidon was the Greek god of the sea, not a fish,' Soul said coldly. 'And who said anything about changing the name of the agency? This is going to be a trial period!'

Reid shrugged. 'I'll grow on you. I think the Hasley and Soul Agency sounds nice.'

Soul scowled. 'Why not Soul and Hasley?'

'Better to go alphabetical. And how much is the rent in Bay Village?'

Soul hesitated. 'I was thinking of moving.'

Reid nodded. 'Good idea. Rent's gotta be cheaper elsewhere.' He looked down at his glass. 'So, you got anything else in this joint apart from whisky? I'm kinda hungry.'

THE END

THE WARRIOR MONK

A SEVENTEEN SERIES SHORT STORY

A.D. STARRLING

IT IS SAID THAT THE BEING WHOM GURU RINPOCHE, THE
Lotus-born Second Buddha, met on his way to the court of King
Dresden stood taller than most men and possessed three times
their strength and speed. It is also said that, though he looked
like a man and spoke like a man, it was clear to Rinpoche that
the stranger was a creature of divine lineage.

Of the many tales the stranger recounted to the Great
Master in the time they spent in each other's company, one
stood out the most.

The story was of a woman born over four millennia past,
who lived for almost half as many years. She was said to have
been the greatest warrior ever born and possessed of
extraordinary battle skills that saw her conquer entire armies
over the centuries of her existence. Her forefathers were
descended from the loins of the very first humans who walked
the Earth and her bloodline was made doubly unique by an
unknown event that granted her kin powers beyond the natural
realm, including the gift of immortality.

One day, sickened by the increasing savagery with which
her clan ruled over the race of man, she rose to defend the weak
and the just, and all those who suffered needlessly at the hands
of the bloodthirsty tyrants who had given birth to her kind.

It was at that time the warrior forged the very first three-
spear weapon upon which the trishula would eventually be
based. The war that followed lasted one hundred days and
nights and turned the sky dark with ash and the land crimson
with blood. On the last day of the fearsome battle, the warrior
defeated the original immortals.

According to the stranger, the descendants of this mighty warrior still walked the Earth and would do so until the End of Days. For her bloodline had a destiny to fulfill, one that been forged in a higher realm, long before all this ever was. The stranger also foretold that a time would come when the warrior's soul would be reborn within the immortal bloodlines, when her skills and valor would be needed the most. The body in which she would reincarnate would be marked with the symbol of her three-spear weapon.

When the Great Master asked the stranger how he knew this, the immortal smiled and said, 'Because I am of the fifth generation born from her bloodline.'

In the decades that followed Guru Rinpoche's encounter with the descendant of the warrior, the Great Master crossed paths with other immortals. He came to believe not only that they stemmed from original divine beings, but also that their existence should be concealed from humankind until such a time that man could accept the reality of their existence without fear.

He thus created a sect of monks whom he tasked with guarding the secret reality of the Crovirs and the Bastians, the two immortal races, and to whom he bequeathed this scripture, the most secret of all his writings. In honor of the immortal warrior whose tale resonated so strongly with him, Rinpoche named his sect the Order of the Three Spears and had them bear a trishula tattoo on their right palm. He also pledged that when the warrior's soul reincarnated, his men would lay down their lives for that immortal.

OCTOBER 2010. TEMPLE OF THE ORDER OF THE THREE Spears. Eastern Himalayas. Tibet.

ABBOT KELSANG STROLLED DOWN THE WINDING, STONE steps to the shallow terrace fifty feet below, where a figure sat in silent meditation.

Mist clung to the trees covering the flanks of the wooded ravine and swirled in ever-changing shapes in the cool currents generated by the fast-flowing river at the bottom of the narrow valley. Jagged stone pillars rose through the shifting white blanket, silent soldiers that had borne witness to the passage of time for eons. The water rushed around the bases of the giant rock formations, streams dividing and merging in an energetic dance before tumbling down the waterfalls to the west of the gorge.

The river was the lifeline of the temple perched high against the cliff side, supplying not only plentiful catches of fish and the water needed to sustain it, but also hydroelectric power to the complex of caves beneath the buildings and the carefully-camouflaged satellite dish in the forest at the summit of the valley.

Abbot Kelsang paused at the bottom of the stairs that had been carved into the rock face hundreds of years before his birth. A smile curved his lips.

A sparrow dozed on the shoulder of the saffron-robed monk sitting on the edge of the cliff. Another one landed on his bald head, pecked his scalp curiously, and flew off into the mist.

'Yonten,' said the abbot.

The monk unfolded his legs and rose to his feet, his

movements so fluid the sleeping bird remained motionless. He turned, pressed his palms together, and bowed.

'Master Kelsang.'

The Abbot was not fooled by his demure voice. 'I saw Brother Ensho limping out of the dojo this morning. You need to be more patient with him.'

The young man flashed his teeth. 'I shall try my best, master.'

The abbot sighed. There was no doubt in his mind that Yonten was one of the best field agents the Order currently had among its ranks. Now twenty-two years of age, he had lived most of his life among the monks of the temple, ever since that day two decades ago, when he was discovered in a nearby forest with his younger brother, Anzan. It was the baby's cries that had alerted a vigilant monk to the presence of the children. With the nearest village miles from the valley, no one could fathom how the two boys ended up alone in the wilderness. After several attempts to trace their family failed to produce any results, the monks concluded the brothers had been abandoned and took them under their wing. Yonten quickly proved his skills both in the classroom and the dojo and became the youngest monk to leave the temple for missions in distant lands.

'I have an assignment for you.'

Yonten's face brightened at the words. The bird blinked, cocked its head at the abbot, and picked its feathers.

'Our enemies are moving once more,' the abbot continued. 'I want you to observe them and report their activities to me.' He narrowed his eyes at the light that flashed in Yonten's eyes. 'You are not to intervene without my permission, is that understood?'

Yonten adopted an innocent expression. 'Of course, master.'

The abbot glanced at the sky. *Oh Heavenly Masters, I sense you sent this one to challenge me.*

'There is time to complete your meditation. Brother Tenzin is gathering the final details of your mission as we speak. You leave at sundown.'

Yonten grinned.

'Our comrades abroad have been warned of your potential need for assistance. Make use of their resources wisely.'

'Yes, master.'

The abbot was grateful for the Order's contacts in both the human and immortal societies – men and women who became temporary novices to benefit from the Order's excellent education before taking up jobs in human society, and immortals who travelled to the hidden valley to explore Tibetan Buddhism and live part of their long lives in peaceful isolation. Most had maintained close relationships with the Order and were keen to assist them in their overarching mission.

The abbot turned and crossed the terrace to the stairs. Halfway up, he encountered a monk coming down the steps. He stopped and smiled gently at the young man.

'Anzan.'

Yonten's younger brother bowed. 'Master.' Anzan's gaze shifted to the terrace. He sighed. 'I see you have told my brother of his mission.'

The abbot looked over his shoulder.

Yonten was doing a highly unmonk-like victory dance

on the terrace, the sparrow flying excitedly around his head.

The abbot grimaced. 'There are days when I wonder what he puts in his yak milk.'

'We all do, master.'

A HOT BREEZE BLEW ACROSS THE MOUNTAIN AND WHIPPED up dust and sand in a yellow veil that dulled the glare of the sun. Yonten covered his nose and mouth with his robe and flattened himself onto the narrow ledge thirty feet from the summit of a cliff.

The sound of heavy drilling echoed across the canyon below him. It came from the tunnel that had been blasted into the rock face some four hundred feet up the opposite wall of the chasm, just ahead and to the right of where he lay. Lines and hoses snaked inside the opening from the portable hydraulic pumps supplying the breakers being used to shatter the rock. A series of platforms connected by ladders ran down the side of the canyon wall all the way to the bottom of the valley, where a crawler crane and three trucks stood parked next to some tents.

It had been a fortnight since Yonten had left the Order and embarked on the reconnaissance mission the abbot had entrusted to him. In that time, he had shadowed their enemy as they travelled from Europe to the remote Eastern Desert Mountains of Egypt.

The men he followed spent the first few days studying a number of narrow, ancient riverbeds before finally starting their excavation into the side of this particular canyon. He gleaned, from watching them use a battery of sophisticated equipment, that they had detected something of interest inside the mountain.

The drilling suddenly stopped. An expectant hush fell across the valley. It was broken by shouts of jubilation. Three men emerged from the gloom of the tunnel and waved animatedly in the direction of the camp.

Five men came out of the tents and looked up the canyon wall. One of them was significantly taller and larger than the other four. Yonten studied the giant figure closely.

Three hundred years had passed since the Order first became aware of the enemy's existence, ever since the latter stormed the temple and stole an ancient artifact that had been passed down generations of abbots. The relic was said to have belonged to a powerful immortal who had bestowed it on the Order for safekeeping many centuries past. Many monks died fighting to defend the temple and many more perished in the blaze that followed when the enemy rained fiery bombs down onto the holy valley where Guru Rinpoche himself once lived. Though they lost numerous precious scriptures that day, the most important ones were saved from the flames, among them the secret writings of the Great Master.

No one knew the true name of their foe. Over the centuries that followed the start of their investigation into the origins and goals of the sect who had attacked them so savagely, the monks came to call them the *Rose Croix*, after the tattoo its members wore on the back of their necks.

The giant man crossed the camp and started climbing the ladders and platforms toward the tunnel. Halfway up, he paused and looked straight at the ledge where Yonten lay.

The monk froze and held his breath. His instincts had been right.

The giant man was dangerous.

He stared across the canyon for several long seconds before resuming his ascent to the tunnel's opening. He disappeared inside with the three men and came out some fifteen minutes later. Standing on the uppermost platform, he slipped a walkie-talkie out of his pocket and spoke into it briefly.

There was movement in the camp. Two of the trucks reversed close to the canyon wall and the men offloaded sections of steel tracks, motorized rollers, metal chains, and a small forklift. They used the crawler crane to lift the equipment into the tunnel.

It was several hours before Yonten finally laid eyes on their discovery. The skin on the back of his neck prickled when two large stone tombs and a smaller box emerged from the opening and were carefully lifted down to the base of the valley.

A strong foreboding filled him as he stared at the coffins. He sensed a dangerous energy coming from them.

Yonten watched the men load the cargo inside one of the trucks. He frowned when two of them disappeared inside the tunnel with a large section of rock-colored canvas. They nailed a similar piece over the outer opening, took down the platforms and ladders, broke camp, and set off toward the north.

Yonten waited until the convoy disappeared around a bend in the canyon before rising to his feet and clambering swiftly up the cliff side. He jogged to the rocky overhang where he had hidden the second-hand motorbike he had used to get to the desert. He tied the small sack containing his belongings around his waist, secured his two staff weapons to his back, and started the engine.

He rode along the cliff top and caught sight of the convoy below him minutes later. The canyon ended after two miles and the trucks and crane ventured out onto the open desert. He made his way down to the plains and followed them. Although he had spray-painted the shiny parts of the bike a dull yellow to minimize reflective glare, he still kept a careful distance from the vehicles.

Evening had fallen when the convoy finally turned into the Port of Safaga. Yonten abandoned the motorbike and watched from the shadows of a depot as the men loaded their precious cargo onto a fishing vessel. He stole onto the boat moments before it left the dock and found a hiding place inside the hold, some thirty feet from where the tombs rested. It was only through a bout of meditation that he managed to suppress the anxiety their proximity engendered.

The boat docked in Port Said at dawn the next morning. Yonten slipped off the vessel and followed the *Rose Croix* sect members as they transported the tombs and the box to a large warehouse close to the waters' edge.

Three days later, the enemy disappeared along with the cargo, in the middle of the night. Neither the Order's intelligence officers nor their contacts in the human and immortal societies could trace where they had gone. Although the abbot ordered him to go to Europe, Yonten decided to return to the Eastern Desert. He was still mystified by the fact the *Rose Croix* sect had masked the tunnel they had dug in the mountain.

He discovered the reason for their clever camouflage when he got there.

A large campsite made of trailers and tents had taken root on the other side of the mountain. He spent a couple of hours observing the men and women working the land with an array of complex instruments before slipping the satellite phone he had been given for the mission out of his robes. He called the Order.

'I thought you were on your way to Germany,' said Tenzin at the other end of the line.

'I took a detour,' said Yonten pleasantly.

Tenzin's tone turned stiff. 'The abbot will be most displeased.'

'I found something interesting.' He updated Tenzin with his latest discovery in the Eastern Desert Mountains. 'Can you find out who these people are? They are not members of the *Rose Croix* sect, this I am certain of.'

'Give me some time,' said Tenzin after a pause.

A trace of remorse flashed through Yonten when he ended the call. He knew full well that he tested the limits of the abbot's patience and that of the other monks in the Order, including his own brother. He suspected he had been similarly challenging to his superiors and comrades in his former lives.

Still, his instincts had never failed him. And right now, they were telling him that something important was happening at the site.

It was a few hours before Tenzin called with the information Yonten sought.

According to official paperwork filed with the Egyptian government, the new arrivals were legitimate archaeologists working for a large, private organization.

It took another day for the Order to discover that the organization was a clever front for the Immortal Culture and History Section of the Crovir First Council, and that it had not only funded this particular dig but dozens of others around the world. Its CEO was none other than the head of the section, a Crovir noble by the name of Dimitri Reznak.

Yonten got his first sight of Reznak two weeks later, on the day the research team finally broke through into another tunnel at the bottom of a shallow valley parallel to the canyon where the *Rose Croix* sect had carried out their excavation. This second passage apparently also led to the place where the tombs and stone box had been for he heard the archaeologists' cries of disappointment and anger when they discovered the *Rose Croix* sect's camouflaged tunnel.

To his surprise, they lowered pickaxes and crates of equipment into the tunnel they had excavated a short time later. He moved closer to the camp and soon gleaned from the scientists' animated conversations that they had discovered a second cave beneath the one where the tombs and stone box had been stolen. A smile tugged at his lips at the news. The *Rose Croix* sect had evidently missed the existence of the other cave.

It was nearly dusk by the time Dimitri Reznak emerged from the opening. He climbed the wall of the valley and stopped at the summit to watch the setting sun, his expression clearly troubled. He made several phone calls as he headed for the Jeep that had brought him to the excavation site.

Yonten watched the archaeologists for a couple more hours before leaving the desert. He made his way to

Europe that very night and staked out the *Rose Croix* sect's known hangouts. What he witnessed troubled him.

The enemy's activities had accelerated dramatically in the last few weeks. Like the abbot, he suspected they were working toward a significant goal, something that would bring major change to the world, and not in a good way.

December 2010. Boston. USA.

Yonten stood behind a tree and watched the apartment block on the opposite side of the road. Movement behind a bay window on an upper floor caught his eye. He glimpsed a slim, shadowy figure.

Even through the glass, he could tell the person he was looking at had an unusual aura. She faded from view.

A month had passed since the events in the Eastern Desert Mountains. Nine hours ago, one of the Order's immortal contacts had alerted Yonten to an interesting development. Dimitri Reznak had assigned an agent of the Crovir First Council to find the artifacts that had gone missing from the cave in Egypt. Her name was Alexa King and she was reputed to be the best special operative the Crovir Council had ever had. Her first task was to travel to Boston and recruit a renowned Harvard archaeology professor by the name of Zachary Jackson to assist her in her mission.

Yonten's instincts, and what he had learned of Dimitri Reznak in the time since he had first learned of the immortal's existence, made him take the first available flight out of Paris, where he had been tracking the *Rose Croix* sect. He arrived in Boston late that morning and headed to an address in the Back Bay area.

By his calculations, Zachary Jackson's apartment was located where he had just seen that intriguing figure. Something told him it was Alexa King. He had likely missed her arrival at the apartment by minutes; according to his source, she had driven from New York to Boston that day. He waited half an hour before exploring the side streets around the block. A black Maserati was parked around the corner from the apartment building.

Yonten smiled. *That's her car.*

He admired the curves of the vehicle before strolling down the road to the next intersection. He stopped by a set of traffic lights. Although he had no intention of interfering with Dimitri Reznak's plans to find the relics that the *Rose Croix* sect had taken from Egypt, Yonten was certain he would cross paths with the agent the Crovir noble had assigned to the mission. He was curious to see who she was and whether she would end up being friend or foe.

He found himself humming while he waited and ignored the stares from passing commuters. It was the height of winter and snowdrifts lined the roads of the city; he no doubt looked strange standing there in his simple saffron robes.

The roar of a powerful engine suddenly rose above the noise of the traffic. Goosebumps broke out across the monk's skin. His senses warned him of a formidable presence drawing near. The black sports car shot into view.

A beautiful woman with short, black hair sat behind

the driver's wheel. A blond man was in the passenger seat. The woman's head turned toward the monk as the car swerved across the intersection.

Their eyes met for a second. Time slowed. The world faded around Yonten.

Her aura was the most incredible thing he had ever seen in his life. Dazzling white flecked with crimson, it spoke of power on a scale he had never before witnessed. And there, rising above her head in a fiery orange glow that almost seared his eyes, was a three-spear weapon. The trishula tattoo on his right palm tingled.

It's her. It's the immortal warrior!

This conviction crystallized in his mind as he watched the car disappear down the road, his heart thundering inside his chest. A voice reached his ears dimly. He blinked and looked at the elderly gentleman who stood staring at him.

'Are you okay?' the stranger asked. 'You look like you've seen a ghost.'

Yonten realized he was gaping in the direction the car had vanished. He closed his mouth, pressed his palms together, and bowed politely.

'I am fine, thank you, sir.'

The old man hesitated, then shrugged and walked away.

The satellite phone rang. Yonten moved under the awning of a building and took the call, his mind still abuzz with what he had just witnessed.

'It's me,' said Tenzin. 'One of our contacts just rang. You need to go to Turkey.'

Yonten gazed across the road and felt the wheels of fate start to turn. 'Why?'

'That big man you told us about, the one you saw in the Eastern Desert Mountains? He's there right now with other members of the *Rose Croix* sect. There's a plane ticket waiting for you at Logan International Airport.'

'Okay.' Yonten hesitated. 'Can you pass a message to the abbot?'

'Yes, what is it?'

'Tell him she is here.'

Puzzled silence fell across the connection. 'Who's here?'

'The immortal warrior we have been waiting for. She has returned to our realm.'

Tenzin paused. 'Did you drink some kind of weird yak milk?'

'No.'

'Then how do you know this?'

'Because I just saw her. She is the Crovir agent Dimitri Reznak has tasked with finding the relics the *Rose Croix* sect took in Egypt.'

'How do you know she's the warrior reincarnated?' Tenzin said, his tone still dubious.

'Auras don't lie.'

Yonten disconnected, a small smile on his lips. His mission had just taken on a whole new meaning, his future now irrevocably linked to the woman who possessed the soul of the immortal warrior. The one whose tale had made such an impression on Guru Rinpoche, all those centuries ago.

YONTEN REACHED ISTANBUL SOME FIFTEEN HOURS LATER and made his way to a nondescript beer hall just off Istiklal Avenue, in the historic district of Beyoglu. It was a little-known *Rose Croix* sect hangout.

He climbed onto the rooftop of the building and moved stealthily to an overhang overlooking a rear courtyard. Barely half an hour passed before two sect members came out for a cigarette. Low murmurs drifted skyward along with thin trails of pungent smoke. Yonten shifted closer to the edge of the roof and caught fragments of the men's conversation.

The name of the giant man was Dragov. From the tone the two sect members adopted when they spoke of him, he was high up in their organization, just as the monk had suspected. It seemed he would be traveling to Port Said the next day.

Yonten thought of the warehouse where the tombs and stone box had been stored for three nights.

He frowned. *Why would they go back there?*

He mulled over this question on his flight to Iskenderun, a city on the southeast Turkish coast. He took the overnight ferry service to Port Said and spent most of the trip meditating in his cabin. By the time the ship docked at the port terminal just after midday the following day, he was still unclear as to the reason Dragov would be returning to the warehouse.

It was while he was making his way through the bustling crowd that his senses alerted him to the presence of the immortal warrior. He looked out over the waters of the canal and spotted a small ferry making its way across from the east bank.

Alexa King's aura was a brilliant white that stood out among the sea of bodies.

Yonten stayed put and watched her disembark with her companion. Heads turned as the pair walked through the crowd. They made an impressive couple, the blond, blue-eyed man at her side as handsome as she was striking. The monk's eyes widened slightly when he registered Zachary Jackson's aura. The Harvard professor was undoubtedly a human possessed of singularly strong will and intellect.

But what fascinated the monk and held his gaze for unblinking seconds was the thread of energy that bound Jackson's aura to that of the immortal warrior. A flash of envy darted through him. The feeling startled him.

It was at that point that Alexa King stopped in her tracks and looked straight at him from the other side of the terminal.

Yonten inhaled sharply and melted into the crowd. King's gaze sought him for several seconds, her eyes scanning the faces inside the terminal with sharp focus. Jackson stopped and said something to her. She hesitated, spoke to him briefly, and started moving through the press of bodies once more.

The monk hung back and pondered what had just transpired. He could not deny his fascination with the woman who bore the soul of the great warrior. What he had not expected was to feel more than just admiration and respect for her. He stared out over the waters of the canal and blushed as he finally put a name to the emotion that had secretly taken root in his heart.

He was infatuated with Alexa King.

Yonten grimaced. There was no way he was ever going

to breathe a word of this to anyone, not even to his brother. He paused as an unpalatable truth dawned in his mind; the abbot would see through him, whether he liked it or not. Which meant he had to work through these confusing feelings before he came face to face with his master. He scratched his head at this vexing development, sighed, and headed slowly for the warehouse.

It wasn't until that evening that he saw King and Jackson again. He was studying the interior of the building through a narrow skylight when he felt her approach from the north. He tore his gaze from the worrying scene unfolding inside the warehouse and shifted to the edge of the rooftop.

King moved silently, her steps fluid as she surveyed the area around the building. Had he not been attuned to her aura, Yonten would not have sensed her presence. She disappeared under the cover of an adjoining depot and materialized a couple of minutes later, her guns in hand and a wary-looking Jackson in tow.

Yonten watched them enter the warehouse through a side door. He moved back to the skylight, peered inside the gloomy interior, and stiffened at what he saw.

Dragov was pointing a gun at the thin, dark-skinned man he had been arguing with for the last ten minutes. Yonten recognized the latter from his last trip to Port Said. The man was some sort of warehouse manager and had been responsible for the tombs' safekeeping. It seemed he was the reason the *Rose Croix* sect had returned to Egypt.

Several sect members stood watch while another two searched the man's desk. The manager sat behind the table, his hands gripping the armrests of his chair as he shouted at Dragov. Despite the evident fear in his expression, it was clear from his body language that he was not cooperating with whatever demands the giant man was making of him.

The gunshot was audible even through the thick glass of the skylight.

Yonten hissed air through his teeth as he watched the manager jerk in the chair. A dark wound bloomed on the man's forehead. He slumped back, his eyes staring unseeingly at the ceiling.

A sudden change came over Dragov and the *Rose Croix* sect members. They froze in unison before looking over their shoulders. Dragov turned and called out to someone.

Yonten squinted in the direction the giant man was staring. He could not see beyond the farthest row of containers and crates that filled the warehouse.

Dragov signaled to the men with him before crossing the floor toward one of the aisles. Two of them climbed onto a pallet and moved stealthily across the top of the packing cases. The other *Rose Croix* sect members vanished in the shadows.

Gunfire erupted somewhere below him seconds later. Yonten felt the immortal warrior's energy surge.

He smiled. *This I have to see.*

He was crawling toward the skylight on the opposite side of the roof when motion near the water drew his gaze. Several men were scrambling out of a van parked farther down the dock. They raced toward the warehouse, their guns drawn.

Yonten rose, drew his jō staff from his robes, and ran lightly across the rooftop. Further gunfire rose from inside the building. He leapt off the edge, somersaulted in the air, and landed lightly in front of the *Rose Croix* sect members when they were several feet from the warehouse doors. They stumbled to a halt, eyes widening and jaws dropping.

He did not give them time to recover. The staff blurred in his grip as he moved between the shocked figures, the weapon striking bone and flesh with loud thwacks. Grunts of pain rose in the night. Guns and fists swung toward his head. He dropped below them, bent at the waist, and delivered a flurry of kicks and blows, spinning inside the tightening circle. Bodies struck the ground around him.

Metal gleamed at the edge of his vision. Yonten leaned back sharply. A sword skimmed past his face. He brought the jō staff up in time to block the next strike and looked down the length of the blade to the man wielding it.

The *Rose Croix* sect member snarled and swung the sword once more.

Yonten deflected the blow, jabbed the staff into his assailant's gut, and brought his leg around in a roundhouse kick that connected sharply with the falling man's face. The sword clattered to the ground. The man's body thudded next to it.

A squeak rose from the side of the building. Yonten dashed around the corner and saw a door swing close behind a sect member. He was moving toward it when an explosion sounded from inside.

Yonten darted through the narrow opening and entered the dark warehouse. Footsteps pounded the ground toward him. He scaled the side of a shipping container and lowered himself atop it just as several figures dashed past in the aisle below. He caught a glimpse of Dragov. The giant man's face was bloodied, his features contorted in a mask of rage.

One of the *Rose Croix* sect members was carrying a rocket launcher.

The dull roar of engines and the squeal of tires rose and faded in the distance outside. Silence fell inside the building.

It was broken by a muffled, rhythmic noise. Yonten rose and ran in a low crouch over the top of the containers toward the direction of the sound.

The rocket-propelled grenade had detonated in the middle of the warehouse, damaging pallets of crates. A tower of boxes had crashed into one of the aisles. The noise was coming from beneath the giant pile, where he could feel King's energy and that of her companion.

Pieces of wood and a cloud of splinters erupted in the air when she broke through their temporary prison. Yonten watched in admiration as she whipped her guns out and surveyed her surroundings with a deadly expression. Jackson climbed to his feet behind her and dusted himself off. He spoke to her briefly. King replied tersely and turned on her heels. Jackson called out after her, shook his head with a defeated air, and followed in her steps.

Yonten watched from a distance as they headed for the office where the dead manager lay. King and Jackson spent nearly an hour searching the desk and filing cabinets crowding the floor before they found something that piqued their interest. The monk hesitated where he crouched in the shadows. Although he would have loved nothing more than to get close enough to hear what they were talking about, he knew King would detect his presence. He waited until they left before going over the contents of the office. His search proved fruitless. Whatever King and Jackson had found, they had taken it with them.

Yonten stood in the middle of the silent warehouse and pondered his next move. He did not doubt he would meet the warrior and her companion soon. It was just a matter of where. In the interim, his time would be best served observing the *Rose Croix* sect. *Are they still in Istanbul?*

There was only one way to find out. He phoned Tenzin. The monk confirmed that there had been an increase in enemy activity at the tavern in Beyoglu.

'Do you need help making your way there?' said Tenzin.

'No.' Yonten hesitated. 'How is the abbot?'

'He is meditating a lot. Something about saving your soul.'

Yonten winced. 'Tell him I shall be in touch again shortly.'

He stole onto a cargo ship bound for Turkey that night and reached Istanbul late in the evening of the next day. Flurries of snow and icy rain fell across the city as he set out toward the Golden Horn. He hunched over the handles of the motorbike he had borrowed from one of the Order's contacts and soon crossed Galata Bridge.

He had just passed Galata Tower when he heard the distant wail of sirens. He slowed and looked over his shoulder. Flashing red and blue lights punctuated the gray haze behind him. They were headed this way. More sirens echoed from the north. Yonten frowned.

He gunned the engine, spun the bike around, and raced up a series of narrow, serpentine backstreets toward Istiklal Avenue. A flickering glow in the sky captured his gaze seconds later. Yonten's pulse accelerated.

He abandoned the bike a short distance from the tavern and ran the rest of the way. The roar of the blaze reached his ears before he saw the flames. He stopped in the shadow of a porch and watched the fire that had engulfed the building, anxiety pulsing through him.

Movement farther up the alley drew his gaze. He froze.

Alexa King was coming down the passage at a dead run. She stopped opposite the burning tavern and studied the blaze with a scowl. Zachary Jackson appeared next to her a moment later.

Yonten's heart slammed against his ribs. He had not expected to meet them again so soon.

He did not have time to ponder the matter of what they were doing there. King's gaze had just landed on him with the focused energy of a deadly laser beam. He turned and ran, adrenaline flashing through his veins.

She gave chase.

They bolted out of the alley and onto a steep road overlooking the Golden Horn. Yonten sprinted down it and flashed a grin at King over his shoulder.

He was rewarded with a glare. Despite the clear danger of being chased by the reincarnated form of one of the most formidable warriors who had ever lived, Yonten could not suppress the wave of exhilaration that flooded him. *This is a fun game!*

He dashed into a narrow side street lined with

restaurants and cafes, looked up at the buildings crowding the passage, and leapt toward a barred window. He gripped the metal shafts and climbed swiftly to a small balcony. He stopped and looked down. King skidded to a stop on the street below.

Yonten gave her an encouraging smile.

She narrowed her eyes, ran down some steps, jumped, and caught a metal beam that ran across the passage. She swung herself up, somersaulted in midair, and landed feet down on the horizontal bar. The crowd below uttered oohs and aahs of amazement.

Yonten dipped his chin approvingly and turned to climb the face of the building. He saw her leap onto an adjacent balcony and ascend along a parallel path to his. He reached the terrace at the top first and leapt across the gap to the next apartment block.

King's footsteps were seconds behind him.

The rooftop chase across Beyoglu lasted several thrilling minutes. By the time Yonten lost her, they had navigated several streets and had travelled almost a mile from the burning tavern. He watched from the shadow of an alley as she studied the cityscape for silent seconds before making her way back toward Istiklal Avenue.

The faint smile on her lips told him she had had as much fun as he during their chase.

YONTEN SPENT THAT NIGHT AT A BUDDHIST CENTER IN THE city. He was getting ready to board a plane to Budapest the next morning when Tenzin rang him.

'Change of plans. We have had word of enemy activity in Italy. I'm changing your ticket to Rome.'

Yonten narrowed his eyes. 'What about the sighting in Budapest?'

'We lost track of Dragov several hours ago. Rome is your best bet to find out what the *Rose Croix* sect is up to next. Our source suspects something big will happen there today.'

Yonten ended the call and looked out over the runways of Ataturk Airport. He could sense dark clouds gathering on the horizon. With the wheels of fate turning faster with the passage of every day, his and the immortal warrior's paths were on a direct collision course with that of their common enemy. The outcome, he feared, would not only be explosive, but would determine the future of humans and immortals alike.

He left Istanbul an hour later and landed at Fiumicino Airport just after midday. The Order's contact in Rome gave him a lift into town.

'Let me know when you're done,' said the former monk.

Yonten bowed and bade him goodbye. He watched the man drive off and turned to gaze at the impressive sight behind him. He was standing in front of a crowded St. Peter's Square. Up ahead, the Basilica glowed under the sun. He started to cross the piazza.

Two gunshots echoed above the hubbub of the mass of tourists filling the giant space.

Yonten froze. His gaze swung to the rooftop of the Basilica just as eerie silence descended on the square. He spotted a dark figure with what appeared to be a sniper rifle positioned behind one of the statues. Panicked screams shattered the frozen stillness. Chaos descended outside the Basilica.

Yonten caught the crack of further gunfire above the noise of the fleeing crowd. This time, it had come from the direction of Vatican Palace. Puffs of plaster and stone chips clouded the air inches from the sniper's position. He pulled back, dismantled his weapon, and disappeared from view.

Yonten felt the immortal warrior's power nearby. He moved under the cover of one of the Tuscan colonnades, tension coursing through his limbs as he scanned the palace. People fled past him, fear evident in their faces. More visitors poured out of the entrances of the Basilica as Vatican police officers and Swiss Guards evacuated the church.

A flash of movement caught his eye. He spotted King and Jackson running on the top of the wing connecting the north colonnade of St. Peter's Square to the Basilica. His jaw sagged.

Someone shot at them.

Yonten's heart leapt into his mouth as King vaulted over a balustrade and jumped toward the bell tower in the Basilica's north portico. She slammed into the railing of the balcony and gripped it tightly before turning and shouting at Jackson. The Harvard archaeologist hesitated before jumping.

King caught his outstretched arm as he fell toward her. Yonten watched incredulously as they swung down the facade of the building to the square. He lost sight of them in the crowd a moment later.

Sirens rose from the direction of the avenue leading to the Basilica. Yonten spotted several Italian police squad cars barreling down the road. Dozens of Vatican police officers and Swiss Guards converged on the center of the square.

Someone fired a shot toward the sky. The crowd parted.

Yonten inhaled sharply. King and Jackson were fighting their way through a growing circle of armed officers. The immortal warrior moved in a fluid dance of lightning-fast kicks and strikes, her expression focused as she engaged their opponents. Her gaze flicked anxiously to her companion.

Yonten unwrapped his sack from around his waist and handed it to a man standing a few feet from him. 'Please dispose of this as you wish.'

The man goggled at him, mouth opening and closing soundlessly.

Yonten smiled. He would have no further need for his belongings. The path he had to take was all too clear. Where it would end he did not know.

Forgive me, master. I know I am not following your instructions, but it is the right thing to do. Guru Rinpoche would approve, of this I am certain.

Yonten took a deep breath, slipped his jō staff from his robes, and bolted across the piazza. He reached the first wave of policemen, slipped through them, and jumped. He somersaulted through the air before landing on the cobblestones in front of King and Jackson. The officers encircling them staggered back. King inhaled sharply behind him.

Yonten smiled at her over his shoulder. His breath caught in his throat. Her eyes were the color of molten silver. The power of her gaze almost brought him to his knees.

He swallowed, took his three-sectional bō staff from his robes, and cast it at her. She caught it in midair.

'Who the hell is he?' hissed Jackson behind her.

King hesitated. 'A friend.'

She stared into Yonten's eyes, dipped her chin, and snapped the staff weapon open. She spun it through a full revolution and whipped it into position beneath her arm.

Warmth flooded the monk's heart at her quiet acknowledgement. He had made the right choice. His place was at the immortal warrior's side from now on, whatever fate had in store for them.

Yonten turned to face the line of stunned police officers and gave them a short, formal bow. 'My most sincere apologies.'

He gripped the jō staff and assumed the basic *aikido* fight stance. The immortal warrior shifted and positioned her back against his.

They moved in perfect unison.

THE END

THE HUNGER

A SEVENTEEN SERIES SHORT STORY

A.D. STARRLING

AUGUST 1695. LIÈGE. SPANISH NETHERLANDS. HOLY
Roman Empire.

CONRAD GREENE STOPPED IN HIS TRACKS, HIS HEART
hammering in his chest. Fifteen feet away, on the opposite
side of a narrow, drab alley, the muzzle of a flintlock
pistol was trained on his head. He kept his hands hanging
loose at his sides and ignored the weight of the twin
pistols and staff weapon tucked in the low of his back.

'Steady there,' he said in a level voice. 'I am only here
to talk, not to fight.'

He was aware of movement on the low roof of the
tannery overlooking the alley to the right. He twitched his
little finger, a silent signal to the man creeping atop the
building. His companion froze.

Conrad studied the shadowy shape wedged in a gap
between two rows of barrels, its back against a brick wall
as it pointed the pistol at him. A new smell reached his
nostrils above the stench of the neighboring workshop
and the foul odor drifting from the nearby River Meuse.
It was the coppery scent of blood.

He registered the absolute stillness of the figure
pointing the firearm and swore under his breath.

'It is all right, Anatole,' Conrad called out to his
companion.

He crossed the alley, crouched in front of the man they
had come to meet, and scrutinized the deep slash in his
throat. Whoever had inflicted the fatal wound had made a
neat job of it, with a single deep arc that had dissected the
man's blood vessels and windpipe. Death would have
been almost instantaneous. The victim had collapsed

where he had been attacked, body trapped between the wooden casks and the fingers of his right hand locked around his firearm in cadaveric spasm. The lack of burnt gunpowder on the pistol indicated he had not had time to fire his weapon.

There was a soft noise behind Conrad as the man on the roof dropped down lightly into the alley. A shadow fell across him and the corpse.

'Bloody hell,' muttered Anatole Vassili, his second-in-command. The red-haired immortal squatted next to him.

'Indeed,' Conrad said, frowning.

This was the second informant who had been murdered since his small group of intelligence operatives arrived in Liège.

Conrad wondered why none of his men had been the subjects of similar attacks. Whoever had killed their sources must have known they had been about to divulge secrets to members of the League of Augsburg, the European Alliance formed in 1686 to counter King Louis XIV of France's aggressive attempts to expand his borders and claim new territories from his disgruntled neighbors following his successful campaigns in the recent Dutch War.

Do they know we are immortals?

He mulled over this worrying thought while he watched his companion pat down the corpse. Anatole paused and leaned closer to the victim.

'There is something trapped in his hand.'

He carefully uncurled the dead man's left fingers. Crumpled in the pit of the latter's palm was a fragment of paper. The immortal lifted it out and unfolded it.

The paper had been ripped from a larger piece. A

section of a red wax seal was visible on the ragged upper-left corner.

'He must have snatched it from his killer,' said Anatole.

Conrad inspected the partial design. He did not recognize it.

Anatole looked at him, his expression hard. 'What do you want to do?'

Conrad tucked the piece of paper inside his jerkin, rose to his feet, and inspected his surroundings, anger coursing through his veins. The chances of there having been a witness to the killing were poor. They had set up the clandestine meeting in a deprived neighborhood on the outskirts of the city, away from curious eyes and ears. Even if someone had seen their informant's killer, they were unlikely to divulge any useful titbits, for fear of reprisal. Although law and order prevailed in Liège, the poor were too often exempt from the protection afforded to the more wealthy citizens. Here, in the back alleys overrun with rats and the smell of human waste, most led a desperate existence well beyond the rules of civilized society.

'Let us return to the inn,' he said stiffly.

They left the dead man where he lay and headed south toward the center of the city. The remains of a fortified citadel rose on the hilltop to the west, its lines sharply defined by the fading sunlight, the crumbling bastions and walls testimony to the bombardment the fortress had suffered at the hands of the French a few years before.

Lights flickered into existence around them as the city's lanterns and fires were lit. They reached the inn where they had taken lodgings and entered the low-roofed tavern on the ground floor. It was already crowded, the air heavy with the unwashed smell of men's bodies and the smoky aroma from the logs burning in the fireplace. They found a small corner table at the back of the room and waited. A hulking figure with pale eyes and an unruly mane of tawny hair finally detached himself from the bar and joined them.

The newcomer took a seat and pushed two tankards of beer toward them. The chair groaned under his weight. 'I sense from your expressions that the meeting did not go well.'

Conrad accepted his drink gratefully and eyed the giant man. Although Horatio Gordian gave the impression of being fat, he knew the immortal was mostly muscle. He had been a victim of the man's vicious bear hugs on more occasions than he could count during their sparring sessions.

Horatio's only family resemblance to Anatole, his younger cousin on his mother's side, was the shade of his hair and the color of his eyes.

'What happened?' Horatio said gruffly.

Anatole grimaced and made a throat-slitting gesture with his thumb. 'Our man suffered a fatal encounter a short time before our arrival.'

Horatio raised his eyebrows, the light from the candle on the table throwing dark shadows on his face. 'Well, that *is* bloody bad luck.' His gaze shifted to Conrad. 'I have had no joy either. About the only interesting thing that happened at the garrison was some idiot infantryman accidentally shot himself in the foot.'

Conrad took a swig of his beer and frowned.

It had been ten days since they were sent to Liège by Victor Dvorsky, their immediate superior and the leader of the Bastian Corps, a growing division of the Order of the Bastian Hunters. Unbeknown to most of the soldiers fighting on behalf of the Alliance, immortals were assisting the monarchs of the League of Augsburg in their attempts to turn the disastrous tide of the war that had started seven years ago.

Few humans knew of the existence of the Crovirs and the Bastians, the two races of immortals who could survive up to sixteen deaths and who had walked among their kind since the dawn of time. Fewer still realized how much influence the immortal societies wielded over human rulers and to what extent they had helped shape mankind's history.

As in many of the human conflicts where immortals were involved, the Crovirs stood firmly on the opposite side of the battlefield to the Bastians and were helping the power-hungry French king in his efforts to annex more land from the Holy Roman Empire. Despite the uneasy truce that had existed between the immortals since the fourteenth century, when their own devastating millennia-old war ended, the two races still had different ideologies when it came to what constituted right and wrong.

With most of the Bastian Corps still stuck at the Hungarian borders assisting Holy Roman Emperor Leopold I with his campaign to push back the Ottoman armies threatening to conquer central Europe from the south, only a few thousand immortals could be spared to fend off the threat from the west. Among them were the freshly-formed groups of intelligence operatives Victor Dvorsky had personally assembled from the best and most unusually skilled soldiers of the Corps. Conrad's company of fifteen men was the first of this strange new breed of agents. As it was, only five of them had come to Liège, including Conrad. The rest of his company were scattered to the four winds along the French borders, where they were garnering essential information for the Bastian First Council.

Three years ago, the Crovirs had helped the French capture the strategically-important city of Namur. Namur sat at the confluence of the Rivers Sambre and Meuse, thirty-six miles to the west of Liège as the crow flies. Five weeks before Conrad was dispatched to this part of the Spanish Netherlands, the League of Augsburg, headed by King William III of England and Maximilian 11 of Bavaria, decided to take the city back. It was a calculated move meant to destabilize the French forces, following the successful recapture of the city of Huy by the Alliance the previous year and the recent death of Louis XIV's most brilliant strategist, Marshal Luxembourg. It was also a desperate measure by the League to re-establish contact with their besieged armies in the Rhineland.

The siege had been going well. In theory, William and Maximilian should either have conquered Namur or been doing so imminently. Three weeks ago, they suddenly found themselves facing a fresh wave of increasingly deadly resistance from the French. A most puzzling situation soon came to light; despite being under siege, the enemy appeared to have mysteriously acquired fresh stocks of a new and powerful gunpowder from an unknown supplier. Victor Dvorsky received an anonymous report indicating the source of the explosives to be Liège. Conrad's mission was to discover how the enemy was getting hold of this gunpowder when their supplies had been cut off by the Alliance.

He studied the dimly-lit tavern. 'Where are Boris and Emil?'

'Here, captain.'

Two figures emerged from the shadows.

The men were of average height and of slender build. They were also twins. Boris was the best tracker in Conrad's company. Emil, his younger brother by ten minutes, was the greatest trickster Conrad had ever met; he once famously conned a member of the Spanish royal court out of a significant sum of money and his daughter's chastity. The only distinguishing feature between the brothers was the faint scar that ran down Boris's left cheek, a legacy from his encounter with a bear when he was sixteen.

Conrad apprised them of the latest grim findings.

'We have nothing new to report,' said Boris.

'Apart from the fact that we are now thoroughly sick of the taste of beer,' added Emil.

'Really?' said Anatole wryly. 'This from the man who once drank a whole cask of the finest German ale and proceeded to throw up over his superior officers.'

Emil belched in response.

The twins had spent most of the last ten days establishing themselves as regular patrons in the drinking houses around the city. They were the ones who had tracked down the men willing to divulge information that could lead to the traitors supplying gunpowder to the French in Namur. Meanwhile, Horatio had infiltrated the local garrison as a farrier in order to glean any useful titbits that could help elucidate the mystery.

Conrad glanced around the room before pulling out the fragment of paper they had taken from the dead man. 'This was in our informant's hand. Does it mean anything to you?'

Horatio and the twins studied the design of the broken seal and shook their heads.

'Darn it all to hell.' Conrad sighed and pushed his chair back. 'All right, I am going to my room. I shall see you in a short while.'

He made his way to his quarters on the second floor of the inn, stripped to his waist, poured cold water from the jug on the dresser into a bowl, and washed the grime of the day off with a cloth. The clatter of horses' hooves and the rumble of carriage wheels on the street outside drifted through the open window. A breeze rattled the shutters and made the flames in the lamp on the nightstand flicker. The Aesculapian snake birthmark on his left forearm appeared to slither in the wavering light.

It was both a symbol and a conduit for his supernatural healing powers, a legacy of his rare, pureblood noble lineage. Although the men he had fought alongside had seen his birthmark and knew of the unique talents associated with it, he kept the snake covered for the most part. His ability to heal not only his own wounds at an unearthly speed but also those of others was not something he divulged readily. Victor Dvorsky and the Bastian First Council knew the truth and did their best to keep it a secret. Public knowledge of his abilities would make him a hunted man and he was far too valuable to their ranks for them to risk him deserting.

A knock sounded at the door. Conrad wiped his face with his hands, grabbed the bath cloth, and waited.

The knock came again. He frowned. His men would have entered by now.

An image of the dead man from the alley flashed through his mind. He grabbed his gilded staff weapon from the dresser next to him, twisted the first ring in the middle of the shaft, and slid his two short swords apart. He slipped behind the door just as it opened.

A shadow fell across the wooden floorboards. Conrad brought a sword up to the neck of the figure who entered the room. The latter froze.

'Is this how you greet your superior officer?' said Victor Dvorsky coldly.

Conrad scowled at the dark-haired man in the doorway and slowly sheathed the swords.

'My superior officer can kiss my sweet—'

A quick flicker of Victor's eyes indicated they had company. Conrad grabbed the edge of the door and yanked it fully open.

A slender figure dressed in close-fitted cotton trousers, calf-length boots, a linen shirt, a loose jerkin, and a cavalier hat stood in the shadowy hall outside his room.

Self-awareness slammed into Conrad and stole his breath as a pair of hazel eyes bore into his soul.

Despite the fact that the figure was convincingly dressed like a man, he knew he was looking at a woman in disguise. The clues were blindingly obvious to any man with a decent pair of eyes.

From the color of her lips and cheeks to the tell-tale swell of her bound breasts, from her narrow waist to the soft, undeniable curves of her hips, she was very much of the female persuasion. A few loose curls the color of roasted chestnuts had escaped the hat and framed her slim neck and jawline.

Conrad was aware that women immortals had been joining the Order of the Bastian Hunters and the Corps since the late 1660s. He had even met several female Hunters when he was at the headquarters of the Bastian Councils in Vienna a few years ago. From what he had heard through his comrades in the Corps, they did as good a job as their male counterparts, if not better. After all, they felt they had a lot more to prove.

Conrad sensed the heat of a leaden stare from his right. He blinked and looked around into Victor's stony expression.

The mesmerizing spell he had fallen under dissipated the instant he lost eye contact with the stranger. He was curiously satisfied to see her inhale shallowly out the corner of his eye, as if she had also been holding her breath.

'Is this going to be problem?' said Victor.

'Is what going to be a problem?' Conrad responded in a dull-witted tone, deliberately pretending ignorance of the sexual tension clouding the air.

Victor looked between Conrad and the woman in the doorway.

She straightened her shoulders, her face filling with steely resolve. 'No.'

Her voice sent hot fingers trailing down Conrad's spine and made the muscles of his belly clench in a way that could only mean trouble.

'This is Sergeant Laurelie Clare Hartwell,' said Victor brusquely. 'As of now, she is part of your company. Laurelie, meet Captain Conrad Greene.'

'I prefer Laura.' She hesitated. 'Captain.'

Conrad tore his gaze from the young woman and frowned at the source of his fresh cause for agitation.

'This is highly unusual, Victor. We are in the middle of a mission. Now is not the time to—'

'The French are bombing Brussels.'

His mentor's words stopped Conrad cold.

'They started last night. We think they are trying to distract the Alliance from Namur.' Victor glanced at Laura. 'Laura gave us enough warning for us to get our people and allies out of there. She also brought fresh intelligence from Paris and Versailles on the French king's future plans. I think she will make a great addition to your company.' He paused. 'And it appears that you need all the help you can get at present.'

Conrad let that remark pass. The news of the attack sent anxiety pulsing through him. He had some good friends in Brussels, most of them human.

'Join us downstairs,' said Victor. 'I've commandeered a private room for our evening meal.'

Conscious of Laura's eyes on him, Conrad shrugged into a fresh shirt and followed the two immortals to the tavern. The innkeeper led them to a small dining room at the rear of the building. Anatole, Horatio, and the twins were already seated at the table and in the middle of enjoying a bottle of wine.

They froze when they saw Victor and rose to their feet.

'At ease,' said Victor.

He turned and introduced Laura. The men's eyes widened as they studied Hartwell.

Anatole opened and closed his mouth soundlessly. 'She is a *woman*.'

Victor sighed. 'Your powers of observation never cease to impress me, Vassili.'

Laura smiled faintly. Conrad wondered whether the others saw the intelligent focus behind her light-hearted expression. Although he was reluctant to admit it, he could see why Victor thought she would be an asset to his company.

A slow grin parted Emil's lips. Conrad stifled a groan; he did not like the keen light dawning in the twin's eyes. He glanced at Laura and was surprised to see her staring unblinkingly at the young man. A tense moment passed. Emil flushed and looked away first.

A jolt of elation darted through Conrad, startling him. Laura Hartwell was evidently not one to shy away from a challenge.

It was only after dinner that he also realized just how perceptive she was.

They had cleared the table and were looking at a map of the Spanish Netherlands and northern France. Laura presented the information she had gathered in Paris over the last few months, pointing out various locations on the chart. Victor watched the other men gathered around the table closely while she spoke. Conrad could not help but feel that his mentor was passing some sort of judgement on how they were reacting to her presence.

Silence fell across the room at the end of Laura's report.

Victor's gaze finally shifted to the young woman. 'Your conclusions?'

It was evident to Conrad that the leader of the

Bastians Corps had already made up his mind about what the intelligence meant.

Laura frowned and hesitated. 'France cannot continue its war efforts at the pace at which it is currently going,' she said finally in a cool, confident voice. 'Even though the king's army outsizes the combined forces of the Alliance, the harvest failures of the last two years have had a significant impact on the French economy and its trading powers. They are running out of supplies. Soon, they will not have sufficient funds to embark on the kind of aggressive, large-scale campaigns we have seen to date in this war. King Louis knows this, which is why his agents have been in talks with the Italians and the Dutch to try and come to some kind of peace agreement behind the Allies' backs. It is also the reason why the French are secretly commissioning private ship owners into service for their country, in an attempt to destroy the Anglo-Dutch naval army.'

Conrad sucked in air at this latest revelation. The French fleet had won some remarkable naval battles in the war effort to date. They could inflict significant damage on the maritime powers of England and the Dutch Republic if Louis's efforts at enlisting privateers proved successful.

'Namur could prove to be the tipping point for this war,' Laura continued. 'If the Allies successfully retake the city and resume communications and supply routes with the Rhineland via the river ways, it would place the French at a critical disadvantage.'

Victor looked at Conrad. 'Your thoughts?'

Conrad studied Laura for several silent seconds. She

stared back just as steadily, the flecks of green in her eyes sparkling in the candlelight.

'I concur,' he said with a curt nod. 'This explains why the French are trying to bolster the gunpowder stocks in Namur with this new explosive.'

He summarized their activities and findings since they arrived in the city.

Victor narrowed his eyes. 'Both informants were murdered?'

'Yes,' Conrad replied. 'It seems whoever the traitor is, he has eyes everywhere.'

'Were you followed when you left the meeting place?' said Laura.

'No.' Conrad glanced at Anatole. 'We split up and took turns shadowing each other on the way back here to make sure a third-party was not doing the same.' He pulled the fragment of paper they had retrieved from the second informant from his jerkin and placed it on the table. 'The only clue we have found so far is part of a symbol.'

Victor and Laura leaned across the table and inspected the seal.

'Does it mean anything to either of you?' Conrad asked.

Victor shook his head. 'No. But I can certainly get our spies in France to look into it.'

Laura pursed her lips.

Conrad tensed, a flicker of hope bursting inside his chest. 'What is it?'

She looked at him blindly, a far-away look in her eyes. 'I believe I may have seen something like this in Versailles,' she murmured. Lines marred her brow. 'But I cannot recall the exact design at this moment.' She ran a hand through her hair. 'Let me sleep on it.'

The matter of sleeping arrangements became an uncomfortable issue an hour later. Victor had departed Liège to return to Cologne and Conrad ordered his men to retire for the night.

'The last room was taken by a merchant late this afternoon,' said the innkeeper apologetically. 'I am afraid you will have to share if you wish to stay here.'

Laura adjusted her hat and lifted the sack containing her belongings. 'I can look for lodgings else—'

'No,' Conrad interrupted sharply.

Her eyes flared slightly at his tone.

'We stay together,' he added gruffly. 'With recent— events, I do not want any of my men to be on their own.'

The innkeeper looked on curiously. Conrad felt a heated stare on the back of his neck. He glanced over his shoulder and saw Anatole watching him with a shrewd expression.

'You can have my room until one becomes available,' Conrad told Laura firmly. 'I will share with one of the others.'

Ten minutes later, he was lying on a pallet on the floor of Anatole and Horatio's room.

'This doesn't feel right, you being the captain and all,' Anatole muttered from where he lay. 'You are certain you do not want the bed?'

Horatio's thunderous snores echoed to the rafters from the other side of the room. The giant immortal had fallen asleep the moment his head had touched the pillow.

'We joined the Corps at the same time,' Conrad said

wryly. 'And we have been friends for decades. I am not sure where this new deference is coming from.'

'It must be because of the latest addition to our group.'

Conrad maintained a diplomatic silence at this deliberate taunt. Anatole grinned.

'What?' snapped Conrad.

'I saw the way you looked at her,' said Anatole.

Conrad's pulse stuttered at his words. *Bloody hell. Was I that obvious?*

'What do you mean?'

Anatole rolled his eyes. 'Do not fret. I suspect I am the only one who noted the fact that you were studying our newest recruit like a starving wolf gazes upon a banquet of the finest meat.'

He blew out the candle on the nightstand and settled down to sleep.

Conrad stared at the dark ceiling. Anatole was wrong. Victor had also detected his visceral response to Laura at their first meeting. He turned on his side and closed his eyes.

Sleep proved elusive. The thought of Laura Hartwell lying naked against the bed sheets he himself had lain on mere hours before kept him awake for the better part of the night.

News of the Brussels bombardment reached Liège by morning and a sombre mood soon fell over the city.

Conrad saw fear in the eyes of the citizens he encountered as he headed toward the docks with Anatole and Laura. The fact that the French were getting closer was not welcome tidings.

Despite Anatole's reassurances that they had cleared the river as a source of the gunpowder contraband, Laura had insisted on visiting the port.

'A fresh pair of eyes never hurts,' she said lightly at breakfast. 'Besides, Victor told me the Bastian Hunters had pretty much ruled out overland transport as a way for the French to be getting their gunpowder supplies. The Allies' blockade has been very effective at interrupting the flow of their other stocks.'

Anatole grunted something indistinct in response.

Laura's decision to inspect the riverside proved more than fortuitous. It was while they were studying the activities on the water from the vantage point of a busy shipping yard late that afternoon that part of the mystery of how the gunpowder was getting to Namur was solved.

Horse-drawn carts trundled up and down the quayside, many taking delivery of the goods that had made their way from Maastricht, while others brought ammunition and rations to be transported upstream to the Allied armies in Namur. One such cart pulled up some twenty feet from where they stood and started unloading wine barrels onto a single-masted Dutch riverboat.

Laura stiffened, her gaze locked on the working men. She uttered a foul swearword under her breath.

Anatole raised his eyebrows. 'Well, that was rather unladylike.'

Laura ignored him. She looked around, grabbed a stick from the ground, and squatted next to a puddle.

Conrad and Anatole exchanged puzzled glances before dropping down on their haunches on either side of her.

They watched as she sketched out a series of shapes in the mud. She finished with a flourish and looked at them with a triumphant expression.

They gazed at her blankly. The animation faded from her face. She sighed.

'The seal,' she explained in the tone of one addressing a pair of idiots. 'It is part of a heraldic symbol.' She indicated the wine barrels across the way. 'Those casks bear a coat of arms. It made me remember the design I saw in Versailles.' She pointed at her drawing. 'A crest of a fish above a coronet. The shield is a field of azure charged with three lions rampant and supported by eagles.' She grinned. 'The piece of paper you collected from your dead informant had the bottom right corner of this design on it.'

Surprise and excitement filled Conrad in equal measure as he stared at the symbol.

He turned to Laura. 'This is excellent.'

His burgeoning smile froze on his lips.

She was less than a foot away. From this close up, he could feel her body heat and see the individual flecks of color in her eyes. They darkened as he watched. Her gaze dropped to his lips, her chest rising and falling with her ragged breathing.

Heat flooded his veins as her scent filled his mind.

'Should I leave?' someone said dryly.

Conrad blinked. Laura inhaled sharply and drew back, almost losing her balance. He was stunned to discover that they had unconsciously leaned toward one another.

Anatole studied them with a lewd smile.

'Has anyone ever told you you are an insensitive ass?' Laura said with a scowl.

Anatole's jaw sagged, shock painted plainly across his face. He burst out laughing in the next moment.

'I hear it all the time,' he chortled. 'From him!'

He indicated a stony-faced Conrad.

The sun's dying rays painted the river crimson as Conrad rose to his feet.

'Come, let us go back,' he grumbled. 'This may very well be the breakthrough we were looking for.'

They met with the others upon their return and told them of their findings. Laura drew out the symbol on a piece of paper and pushed it to the middle of the table.

'We need to find out whether anyone uses this design in the city,' she said, tapping the paper with her finger. 'I suspect the person or persons supplying the French with this new gunpowder may very well reside here, in Liège.'

Horatio rubbed his chin thoughtfully. 'That would make sense. They would know this area well.'

'We still don't know *how* the supplies are getting to Namur, though,' said Boris.

'One thing at a time, brother,' said Emil.

His face shone with admiration as he stared Laura.

Conrad narrowed his eyes.

'Now, now, he is just showing his appreciation,' Anatole muttered next to him.

Conrad was not so sure. He sensed Emil wanted to do much more than that to Laura Hartwell.

His fears came true hours later. Having decided to start their search at daylight, they were having a few late night drinks when Emil made a grave mistake.

Although Laura had kept up with their drinking, consuming as much beer as any of the men at the table with cool composure, Conrad detected tiredness in her bearing and her eyes. He pondered the amount of traveling she had done to bring information to Victor and the Bastian Councils.

She has probably not had a full day's rest for over a week.

Laura excused herself presently and rose from the table. 'I bid you good night.'

Emil reached out and grabbed her arm as she turned from the table.

'Wait! It is far too early for you to go to sleep,' he said in a slurred voice. 'Come, stay and have another drink.'

Conrad frowned. *I should have stopped him drinking two beers ago*, he thought belatedly.

'No, thank you,' Laura said in a polite but firm tone.

She took hold of Emil's hand. His grip tightened around her arm.

Silence descended across the table. Everyone's eyes focused on where Emil's fingers lay on Laura's skin.

Conrad started to rise from his chair. A quick flicker of Laura's eyes curbed his motion. The intention he read in her glance was clear.

Let me handle this, it said emphatically.

She took a step toward Emil and leaned down slightly.

'Are you certain you want to do this, little boy?' she said in a voice that sent alarm bells ringing in Conrad's mind.

'Oh brother,' Anatole murmured beside him. He had evidently picked up on the dangerous undertone in Laura's words, as had everyone else at the table bar Emil. 'She *does* know he has about one hundred years on her, right?'

Conrad did not reply, his gaze focused on the frozen picture of the man and woman across the way. How this ended would determine how Laura Hartwell would be regarded by the men in his company.

'He is about to get his ass kicked,' Horatio murmured.

'Amen,' Boris concurred, shaking his head. 'He deserves a good kicking. I am ashamed to call him my brother right now.'

Emil blinked and glanced at them with a befuddled expression, oblivious to the lurking danger. He grinned at Laura and tugged on her arm.

What followed happened so quickly it made Conrad draw a sharp breath.

Laura hooked one foot under the front leg of Emil's chair at the same time that she used the weight of her body to push him back. Emil's eyes widened comically when the chair toppled backward. He reflexively pulled on her arm as he started to fall. She was expecting it and moved with him, her motion fluid and controlled.

Emil let out a shout as they crashed to the floor.

Laura straddled his chest, gripped his throat with one hand, and reached behind her back with the other.

'I believe you owe me an apology,' she said silkily in the frozen hush.

At this late hour, the tavern was almost deserted. No one outside their group witnessed the dramatic events unfolding at their table.

Proving once and for all that he was an utter fool when under the influence of alcohol, Emil leered drunkenly and ran his hands up the outside of Laura's thighs to her hips.

The sight made Conrad want to stab the young man repeatedly in the heart, regardless of the fact that he would rise again by virtue of his immortality.

A small sigh left Laura's lips. There was a blur of movement.

Emil went deathly still as the edge of a blade kissed his neck. She leaned in and pressed her dagger into his flesh, drawing a drop of blood.

'I still think you want to tell me something.'

Emil swallowed, suddenly sober.

'Hmm. I am sorry,' he mumbled.

Laura cocked her head. 'I am sorry?'

Emil glanced at the men at the table in confusion. His brother mouthed the magic words to him.

'I am sorry, Sergeant Hartwell,' the younger twin said in rush of words.

Laura withdrew the blade, tucked it back in its sheath, and rose smoothly to her feet.

She gazed steadily at Conrad. 'I hope this does not constitute assault against another officer, captain.'

'Er, no.' Conrad did his best to mask his grin. 'I would say it was appropriate defense against the actions of an imbecile.'

Laura nodded curtly and disappeared in the direction of the stairs. Conrad suspected he was the only one who saw the faint trembling of her hands.

'I like her,' said Anatole with a grin.

On the other side of the table, Boris helped his brother up and slapped him around the head.

It was Emil who discovered the identity of the seal's owner the next day. Conrad, Laura, and Anatole were in the administrative quarters of the city, where they had spent several hours subtly questioning dozens of government clerks, when the twin found them. He was not alone.

Conrad straightened when he saw Horatio and Boris behind Emil.

'Did you find something?' he said stiffly.

Emil nodded, his expression hesitant as he glanced at Laura. She gave him an encouraging nod.

'The man we are looking for is Baron van Haghen, a nobleman and a cousin of Louis XIV thrice removed,' said Emil. 'One of the tavern girls recalled seeing the heraldic symbol Sergeant Hartwell drew for us on the scabbard of a sword. It belonged to one of the baron's men. He is a nasty piece of work, apparently.'

'I did some footwork and found out a bit more,' said Boris. 'van Haghen resides in a mansion in the hills to the west of the city. In addition to the wealth he inherited from his forebears, he manages several successful trading businesses.'

'Overland?' said Conrad sharply.

Boris nodded and grinned. 'And by riverboats. He is one of the main suppliers of the Allies in Namur.'

Conrad looked at Laura. 'It seems you were right after all.' He frowned. 'But if he is providing provisions to William and Maximilian, how the devil is the gunpowder getting through to the French?'

'I asked at the garrison,' said Horatio. 'He has a shipment of rations going to Namur tonight.'

THEY LEFT FOR THE DOCKS NORTHWEST OF THE CITY AT dusk and took up position in a narrow alley close to the water. A large galliot boat was moored on the quay thirty feet from where they crouched in the shadows. A line of carts stood parked on the riverside next to the vessel.

'I can't see anything out of the ordinary so far,' murmured Conrad after a while.

'And by the looks of things, the Allies in Namur have tightened their security,' said Anatole.

A group of men were loading barrels and sacks from the carts onto the boat. They did so under the eyes of a government official evidently charged with supervising the transfer. The clerk carefully checked and ticked off each item on his manifest.

As they watched the last barrel go aboard, a clatter of hooves drew Conrad's gaze to the right. A man drew up on a horse next to a cart and dismounted. He handed the reins to one of the men charged with stocking the ship, spoke to him briefly, and strolled up the gangway onto the boat.

'That man fits the description the tavern girl gave me,' murmured Emil.

The vessel slipped its moorings a moment later and headed south in the direction of Namur, oars silent and sails taut in a prevailing wind blowing from the north.

Frustration gnawed at Conrad as he watched the boat drift silently along the waterway. 'The goods will likely be checked at their final destination as well.'

'If van Haghen is the one getting the gunpowder to the French, then he must be using sorcery,' said Horatio.

'Not necessarily,' said Laura.

Conrad turned and gazed into her gleaming eyes.

'That stretch of river is more than thirty miles long,' said Laura. 'A lot can happen in thirty miles. Especially under the cover of darkness.'

Emil's eyes widened. 'You mean—'

'They could stop that boat at any stage before Namur and load more goods on board,' said Laura.

Horatio frowned. 'The stocks would still get checked by the Allies at the other end.'

Laura stared at the water, a far-away look in her eyes once more.

Conrad was starting to recognize that expression. It meant cogs were turning in her clever mind.

'Not if they hide them,' she finally murmured.

Horatio scoffed. 'Where would they hide them on a boat?'

A dangerous smile floated on Laura's lips.

A thrill shot through Conrad. He had just arrived at the same conclusion he suspected she had already reached.

'Not on the boat,' he said slowly. '*Under* it.'

Laura nodded in agreement, her gaze focused sharply on his face. 'Those boats are unlikely to return immediately. If they dock close to the Allies' pontoon bridges, the men could slip into the river and float barrels of gunpowder underwater to the French side in the dark. The siege will be a noisy place. The soldiers are looking out for boats trying to cross over to the enemy's side. They are unlikely to notice much else.'

Silence greeted her explanation.

'That is clever,' Anatole said darkly.

'There is only one way for us to see if our theory is correct,' said Conrad.

Laura's face hardened with anticipation. 'We have to follow those boats.'

They retrieved their horses from the inn's stables and headed off briskly down the west bank of the River Meuse. They did not have far to go. Five miles from Liège, beyond a small hamlet and a curve in the river, they came to a stop on the brow of a low hill.

They dismounted swiftly, secured their horses under some trees beyond the dirt path, and headed quietly down the slope toward the riverbank.

The baron's boat had dropped anchor in the middle of the waterway. Lanterns shone on the deck of the vessel. Shadows moved in the yellow light.

Conrad and his company entered the line of trees bordering the river a moment later. They stopped in the shadows and observed the stationary carts on the embankment some thirty feet away.

A pair of skiffs was making its way from land toward the boat, bottoms heavy with barrels. Two men stood at the water's edge, their attention focused on the activity on the river.

The skiffs reached the port side of the boat. Shadowy silhouettes toppled barrels into the water and slid in after them. They disappeared beneath the vessel.

Boris glanced at Conrad and Laura. 'You were right.'

'Clever bastards,' said Horatio.

'What do you want to do?' said Anatole.

Conrad looked around. The red-haired immortal was grinning at him, his pale eyes gleaming menacingly.

'We could leave and let Victor and the Allies know of our findings,' he said slowly. 'Or we could stop these men here.'

Other deadly smiles broke out in the gloom. Conrad's lips twitched.

Despite the fact that they were outnumbered, he never doubted his men would be up for the challenge. From the expression on Laura's face, she was just as keen to stop the enemy.

They slipped from the shadows seconds later and silently disposed of the men by the carts. They dragged the bodies under the trees before splitting up. The twins stayed on the embankment. They were of the same build as the dead men; in the dark, they would easily be mistaken for them. This would hopefully buy Conrad and the rest of them enough time to attempt the foolhardy plan they had just concocted.

Conrad ran swiftly along the bank with Anatole, Horatio, and Laura. They entered the river some forty feet south of where the boat floated in the water and swam toward it with the current, making sure to stay on the starboard side.

They were fifteen feet shy of the hull when one of the skiffs started to make its way back toward the embankment where the carts stood. Conrad scowled and hastened his strokes.

Their time was about to run out.

He reached the stern of the vessel, grabbed the anchor rope, and climbed up it rapidly, the others close behind him. Water dripped off him in rivulets when he stepped noiselessly onto the deck. He reached for his staff and unsheathed his swords, feeling somewhat vulnerable without his pistols.

They had hidden their firearms under some trees on

the bank of the river. Without watertight bags in which to carry the weapons, there was no point bringing them.

Horatio was the last one to come aboard. Anatole was just helping him over the gunwale when shouts broke out from the direction of the west embankment. The sounds of clashing swords followed.

Conrad signaled to the others and stole into the cover of the stacks of barrels crowding the deck. He headed toward the middle of the boat, Laura following close in his footsteps. Anatole and Horatio moved along a parallel path on the port side.

Someone stepped out of the gloom ahead of Conrad just as he reached the level of the mast. A blade arced toward his neck. He blocked it with his sword and took a step back. There was movement behind him as Laura slipped into the gloom between two rows of casks.

The man Emil had pointed out on the quayside in Liège stood facing Conrad. Two of his men came up behind him, their swords drawn.

'I see you and your rats have finally come out to play,' the stranger said with an evil smile.

Conrad knew instinctively that he was looking at the person responsible for murdering the two informants.

'Your baron is not exactly being faithful to the cause he pledged himself to.'

The assassin shrugged. 'Philip owes a blood tax to Louis.' His smile widened. 'Besides, he wants to see the Alliance burn and the Sun King take his rightful place as the head monarch of Europe.'

Men cried out and swords clanged on the other side of the deck. An explosion sounded as a pistol was fired.

'That is not going to happen,' Conrad said calmly.

A shadow had slipped behind one of the men at the stranger's side. Metal gleamed under starlight.

The man let out a gurgle and folded to the deck, his hand at his throat. Blood spurted from between his fingers.

Crimson tainted the edge of Laura's dagger where she stood over him.

'A *woman?*' the second man shouted in horror.

Laura had left her hat on the river's bank. Without it, the knot of luxuriant hair at the back of her head was visible.

She sheathed her dagger and brought her rapier up to attack the shocked man. He raised his own sword in defense.

Conrad engaged the baron's assassin as the latter swung his blade at him. Out the corner of his eyes, he saw Laura dance circles around her opponent. She had just disposed of him when a third man slunk up at her back.

Conrad deflected a deadly strike to his chest and opened his mouth to shout out a warning. He need not have bothered.

Laura glided out of the way of the silent attacker's sword and turned to face him.

Metal suddenly hummed past Conrad's face. He swore and jumped back a step, his attention focusing on his own battle once more.

Laura Hartwell had more than proven that she could take care of herself.

It was several minutes before Conrad finally saw an opening. By then, Laura had disappeared to help Anatole and Horatio on the other side of the boat. The assassin snarled and thrust his sword at Conrad's heart. The immortal dropped beneath the blade and brought his own twin swords up. They met the man's arms just below his shoulders, carving through muscles and tendons almost to the bone.

The assassin gasped, his partially-severed arms dropping uselessly to his sides. Conrad crossed his blades and slashed the sides of the man's neck, almost decapitating him. The assassin stared at him in glassy horror before dropping to the deck.

Conrad stepped over his body and made his way across the boat.

He reached the port side in time to see Anatole stab the last standing man in the chest and push him overboard. A crash sounded from below as the body landed on something solid. Conrad looked over the gunwale and saw the bow of the skiff tip up, dumping the men inside and their precious cargo into the river.

He gazed anxiously toward the riverbank and heaved a small sigh of relief.

Emil waved at him from the waters' edge. Boris was divesting the bodies on the ground of their weapons.

'That went better than I thought it would,' someone said beside Conrad.

He looked around and saw Horatio fingering a long cut on his arm. Although the wound was not serious, Conrad walked over to him and laid his left hand on the gash. Warmth flooded his chest as his healing powers surged. A line of heat traveled along the body of the Aesculapian snake before disappearing into the flesh beneath his fingertips.

The wound healed before his eyes, muscles and skin knitting seamlessly together.

'Thanks,' Horatio mumbled.

Conrad sensed a hot gaze on his face. He looked around and saw Laura staring at him with an unfathomable expression.

Crimson stained her shirt at her collarbone.

'Let me take a look at that,' he said, taking a step toward her.

She took a step back.

Conrad stopped in his tracks, feeling strangely hurt.

'I suspect Victor warned you of my abilities before you came to Liège,' he said in a neutral voice.

Laura hesitated before dipping her chin.

'There is no need to be afraid,' said Conrad. 'I will only expedite your body's natural healing process.'

He read her acquiescence in her expression and took another step toward her. This time, she stood her ground.

Conrad stopped before her and carefully moved the collar of her shirt aside. The wound stretched from her collarbone to the rising swell of her breast. He inhaled shallowly and raised a hand to her flesh.

If she noticed his shaking fingers, she did not comment on it.

Her skin scorched his hand. Heat exploded along his arm. A river of fire flooded his body, erasing all coherent thought in its path. Visceral hunger gripped Conrad and made his belly contract.

Laura's cheeks flushed and her pupils widened. He saw the same gut-wrenching need reflected in the hazel depths. She started to rise on her tiptoes, a small moan escaping her lips.

The passionate sound brought him crashing down to

the reality of the moment. He gasped and stepped back, his hand dropping at his side.

Laura froze. Shock flared across her face as she realized what had almost happened. She pulled the collar of her shirt closed, suddenly looking vulnerable.

'That—that should do,' stammered Conrad, his pulse racing.

He had healed her wound before he broke contact.

A muffled curse rose behind him. He looked over his shoulder and saw Anatole drag a man out of the hold, Horatio in his steps.

'Guess who I found hiding like a rat aboard his own ship?' said Anatole with a grin. 'The captain no less. He should be able to testify to the authorities in Liège regarding the baron's activities.'

They fished the rest of the baron's men from the river and tied them up in the hold. Emil and Boris brought the remaining barrels over in the skiff and they loaded them onto the boat before setting sail for Liège. They left the casks secured beneath the vessel where they were.

It was late morning by the time they returned to the inn. It had taken Conrad several hours to explain his mission findings to the head of the garrison and the nobles in charge of the local government before his company handed the vessel and the prisoners over to them. Soldiers were sent to arrest the baron.

By the time Conrad and his company finished their late breakfast, rumors of the treacherous act had started to spread through the city.

'You should all get some sleep,' said Conrad as he rose from the table. 'We will be returning to Cologne tomorrow.'

Grumbled protests broke out among the men.

'Let us at least stay here another two days,' said Emil with a pout.

'I could do with resting my aching bones,' Horatio concurred, rubbing his chin.

'And Boris has unfinished business with one of the tavern girls,' said Anatole with a sly grin.

Conrad cocked an eyebrow at the blushing twin.

'All right,' he muttered with a sigh. 'Two days it is then.'

The innkeeper came over. 'There is a room available if the young—man still wishes to use it.'

Laura's disguise had evidently not fooled him.

'Thank you,' she murmured.

She followed the man up the stairs.

Conrad waited a good fifteen minutes before slowly making his way to his room.

Though it was empty of her belongings, her scent still lingered in the air. He stared at the rumpled sheets on the bed, closed his eyes at the torrid images that flashed through his mind, and brought his things over from Anatole and Horatio's quarters. He walked across to the window and leaned on the sill, his thoughts full of the events of the last few days.

He was still staring out over the city when a faint knock came at his door. His pulse jumped.

'Come in.'

Laura walked in and closed the door behind her. She turned the key in the lock and leaned back against the wooden panel, her gaze steady on him.

Conrad straightened and turned to face her.

They both knew what was going to happen. He recognized it in her expression. They had known it from the second they first laid eyes on each other. Now that the mission was over, they could no longer ignore the mystifying, burning attraction between them.

Conrad tried to tell himself that this was a bad idea. That a relationship with a subordinate would be frowned upon. He recalled his father's words about never mixing the pleasures of the flesh with work. He imagined Victor Dvorsky's expression when he found out the truth, which he would inevitably do.

All those concerns fled from his mind when he looked at the woman in front of him. As incomprehensible as it was, he could not deny the deep-seated, all-consuming hunger he felt for her.

'I believe you know why I am here,' said Laura.

Conrad nodded, suddenly tongue-tied.

'You know when we first met and Victor asked whether this was going to be a problem?'

She crossed the room and stopped before him.

Conrad swallowed at the light burning in her eyes, green glowing on a sea of gold.

'I lied,' she whispered.

THE END

THE BANK JOB

A SEVENTEEN SERIES SHORT STORY

A.D. STARRLING

The rumor first reached his ears late one Wednesday night. Howard Orson Rodney Titus looked up from his third glass of whisky and glanced casually at the mirror opposite the bar. Outside, a cold autumn wind blew in over the city from Lake Michigan and rattled the windows faintly.

The drinking club was one block from the Chicago Board of Trade, on West Jackson Boulevard. It was a prime destination for the brokers who worked the Pit, the trading floor of the world-renowned institution. Here, they would share tales from their busy day, boast about the deals they had negotiated, and lament the ones they had lost.

A man with a good ear and a sharp mind could learn a lot from listening in on their conversations.

Howard was one such man. In the six months he had been coming to the club, he had already made more than a million dollars investing in stocks and commodities through several phantom corporations.

He sipped his drink and focused his attention on the two men sitting in the red, velvet-lined booth behind him. One was more rake than man. The other was short and portly, with an abundance of facial hair that gave him the appearance of a walrus.

'You sure about that?' said the Rake with a dubious expression.

The Walrus nodded vigorously, double chins wobbling. 'As God is my witness, that's what my cousin Larry told me. And he should know, he works there. The higher-ups are denying it, but the rumor mill is rife with speculation about the transfer.'

The Rake cocked an eyebrow. 'Why would the New York Federal Reserve Bank move that much gold and cash to the First Chicago Bank?'

'It's the Liberty war bonds,' said the Walrus. He glanced around the bar, leaned toward the other man, and dropped his voice slightly. 'Washington has raised more than fifteen billion dollars to fund the country's war efforts since it started issuing them in April. Most of the currency is cash and gold flowing in from Europe. The reserve banks are expanding their strongrooms to accommodate the influx. First Chicago is a charter member of the Federal Reserve system. It had a brand new steel-reinforced concrete vault installed in its basement last year. New York Federal Reserve wants to use its storage capacity for the next two months while it has its own vault modified.'

A nervous chuckle escaped the Rake. 'Better not let any thieves hear about it, then. They'd be over the place like vultures on a carcass.'

The Walrus shrugged and sat back in his seat. 'I doubt anyone will be able to get in that vault. From what Larry said, it's a beast.'

Howard smiled faintly into his glass. Unfortunately for the First Chicago Bank, the Walrus and the Rake's conversation had just been overheard by one of the most talented thieves and con men in the whole of Europe and the Continental United States.

He pondered what the Walrus had said about the vault. *Now, there's a challenge.*

It had been some time since he last committed a

physical act of burglary. With the rise of the stocks and commodities markets both in the United States and abroad, he had been trying his hand at a less dangerous way of making money for the last five years. The fortune he had amassed to date technically made him one of the richest men in the Midwest. He could choose to retire tomorrow and live out the next sixty years in the lap of luxury.

Except that he would live much, much longer than sixty years.

Maybe it's time to see if I've still got what it takes.

A thrill shot through him at the thought. He finished his drink, left a generous tip for the bartender, walked past the booth where the Rake and the Walrus sat talking about their plans for the coming weekend, and exited the club.

NOVEMBER 1917. CHICAGO.

HOWARD SHIVERED AND TUGGED THE COLLAR OF HIS COAT closed. Snow drifted silently from the gray skies, dusting his fedora with soft flakes. He shoved his gloved hands inside his pockets and huddled against the wall of the alley. One hundred and fifty feet northeast from where he stood, across a busy junction crowded with noisy automobiles and electric streetcars, stood a towering building.

The First Chicago Bank was housed in an impressive neoclassical construction over twelve stories tall, on the corner of Washington and State Street. The edifice was but one of many such skyscrapers that had sprouted up all over the cities of Chicago, New York, Philadelphia, Detroit, and other major players in the last three decades. Made of a steel-framed skeleton clad in cream-colored masonry, it allowed for rows of large, plate-glass windows that extended all the way to the elegant cornice crowning its roof some one hundred and fifty feet above the ground.

Not only did Howard know the exact physical layout of the entire building, he also knew all its entry and exit points. A carefully hand-drawn copy of the floor plans was tucked inside his coat, courtesy of an illegal nocturnal trip to the city's planning offices some three weeks ago.

He glanced at his watch.

It was ten to four in the afternoon. He had been watching the place for five hours and had already completed two full surveys of the comings and goings in the building, including the services and goods entrance to the north. It was time to make his move.

He picked up the briefcase by his feet, adjusted his hat, and headed across the street toward the bank's entrance.

A grand hall dotted with Corinthian columns and capped by a magnificent, sculptured, coffered ceiling with crystal chandeliers opened out beyond the main doors. Dozens of customers and clerks occupied the polished-wood counters and rows of desks lining the white marble floor, their voices filling the vast space with a low rumble.

It was a Friday and the end of the month. This made it one of the bank's busiest trading days. It was for that very reason he had chosen this date for what he intended.

Howard walked straight through the lobby to the

elevators at the back, his steps brisk and confident, his expression that of a man on a mission. He ignored the casual glances of the two armed guards watching over the hall and entered one of the elaborate metal cabins. The ride to the seventh floor took mere seconds in the high-speed elevator. For the hundredth time, Howard marveled at the remarkable technological breakthroughs of the last few decades as he strolled down a corridor with a vaulted ceiling.

Human society had come a long way in the last fifty-four years. The fact that other, not-quite-so-mortal beings were responsible for the most significant scientific and engineering advances of the Industrial Revolution that started in the mid-seventeenth century was not something most humans were aware of. He recalled his own humble origins in the British Columbia settlement of Gastown, now known as the city of Vancouver. The last time he visited the place was over two decades ago, after it was rebuilt following a terrible fire that had consumed it in a matter of minutes. He had barely recognized the town of his birth.

Sadness clouded his mind for a moment at the thought of his parents. Though he was an only child, he had become estranged from them following their ardent disapproval of his decision to leave British Columbia. When they realized how he was earning his living, they had, for all intents and purposes, disowned him.

He crossed the width of the building, turned the corner at the end of the passage, and soon reached an anteroom. A secretary sat behind the reception desk, her head bowed as she spoke quietly into a candlestick telephone. She looked up when he stopped in front of the table.

Howard took his hat off and smiled.

The woman blinked, stammered a hasty goodbye into the mouthpiece, and placed the receiver back on its hook.

'Good afternoon,' she said breathily, a faint blush coloring her cheeks. 'May I help you?'

Howard was well aware of the impact his features and build had on the fairer sex. He had used his looks to their full advantage ever since he turned fifteen and lost his virginity to a widow who lived down the street from him. Of course, none of the women he had courted over the years knew his real age. To them, he appeared to be an unusually charismatic and handsome man in his twenties. The fact that he was in the fifth decade of his existence would have shocked any one of them into a fit of vapors.

'I have an appointment with Mr. Thomson.'

The secretary inspected her organizer and scribbled an entry into it. 'Mr. Thomson is expecting you. Let me show you to his office.'

She rose from the desk and led him toward a passage on the left, her hips swaying slightly more than strictly necessary under his amused gaze. Four doors lined the narrow hall they entered. A fifth stood at the end of it; it was made of steel and bore a Yale bank lock.

The secretary knocked on the second door to the right and ushered him over the threshold.

'Mr. MacMillan is here for his four o'clock appointment, sir,' she said demurely to the gray-haired man behind the wide walnut and oak desk that took pride of place in the elegantly-furnished room.

Thomson looked up from the paperwork in front of him, took his spectacles off, and stood up.

'Thank you, Mary.' He came around the desk and extended a hand to Howard, a polite smile pasted across his face. 'It's a pleasure to meet you, Mr. MacMillan. I believe you are here to deposit some bonds?'

'Indeed I am.'

Howard shook the bonds manager's hand before taking the seat the man showed him to. He opened his briefcase, removed a thick envelope from inside, and passed it across the desk.

Thomson placed his spectacles back on his nose and opened the envelope. His brown eyes widened slightly as he studied its contents.

'These are quite substantial bonds, Mr. MacMillan.'

Howard sat back in the chair. 'That they are. To the tune of a quarter of a million dollars, to be exact.'

Thomson hesitated. 'They look new. May I ask how you acquired them, sir?' An awkward expression flashed across his face. 'I'm sorry, but it is our bank's policy to ask this question when such a large sum is involved.'

Howard smiled. 'That's quite all right. Let's just say that I have uncanny luck when it comes to investments.'

The certificates Thomson currently held in his hands constituted a fifth of the bonds Howard had acquired on the stock and commodities market in the last few months. Their value just exceeded the limit required to open a high-asset safety deposit box in the bonds vault at the end of the corridor outside the manager's office.

He had learned this from a First Chicago Bank clerk he befriended two weeks previously in a bar around the corner from the building. The man had been agreeably talkative, especially after Howard had slipped some scopolamine into his drink. The drug had been used for a number of years to produce an amnesic condition in women during childbirth, whereby they would remain conscious but not experience or remember their labor pain. One of its more unusual side-effects was that the person under its influence answered all questions truthfully and wouldn't recall any conversation they had had once the medication wore off.

In addition to providing Howard with information on how to secure a safety deposit box in the bonds vault and describing the lock mechanism on the door, the clerk also volunteered Thomson's name.

'All that's left to do is to fill in the paperwork,' said Thomson presently, removing some forms from a drawer and picking up his ink pen.

It took ten minutes to complete the registration documents. Howard signed his fake name with a flourish and waited patiently while Thomson asked his secretary to procure a safety deposit box key. At half past four, the bonds manager led him to the vault outside his office.

Howard glanced around the room, an appropriately curious expression on his face. The chamber was twenty by fifteen feet and featured a white marble floor, sculptured coving, and a large chandelier. Wide steel cabinets containing rows of safety deposit boxes were securely fixed against two walls. A table and chair stood at the far end of the room, opposite the vault door. Howard's gaze dropped briefly below the table. He bit back a smile.

'This is your safety deposit box.'

Thomson had stopped in front of the middle cabinet

on the left. Howard took the key he offered and placed the bonds inside the box the manager indicated.

'Just one more form to sign,' said Thomson as he headed for the exit.

Howard slipped his hand inside his coat pocket as he followed in the man's footsteps. He took out a slim, cigarette box-sized metal device with a magnetic attachment and stuck it surreptitiously against the inbuilt panel containing the time lock and vault alarm, on the inside of the vault door. He depressed the small button atop the contraption just as Thomson twisted around to close the door.

They headed back to the manager's office, where Howard completed the final paperwork under the man's watchful gaze.

'It's been a pleasure doing business with you, sir.' Thomson glanced at the grandfather clock in the room as he shook Howard's hand.

It was a quarter to five.

'Same here,' said Howard with a sincere smile as he collected his hat and briefcase. 'I hope to see you—oh, I'm sorry.'

Thomson picked up Howard's hat from the floor and handed it to him. 'It's quite all right.'

'Thank you.'

Howard left the man at the door, strolled out into the anteroom, and tipped his hat at the secretary on his way out. He whistled a tune under his breath as he made his way toward the other side of the building, his relaxed demeanor masking the steady rise of his heartbeat. The corridor around him slowly filled up with people, the bank staff finishing up for the day to head home for the weekend. In the crowd of bodies heading for the elevators, no one noticed him when he slipped through a fire door.

The stairwell beyond was narrow and functional, a sharp contrast to the grandeur of the public areas of the bank. Howard headed briskly up the steps. Six levels up, the staircase ended at a rooftop door. It was the only one of the four fire escapes in the building that had direct access to the roof.

Howard opened the briefcase and carefully lifted out the cover of the secret compartment at the bottom. Packed tightly inside were a pair of moccasins with elk skin soles, a coil of climbing rope, a pouch of carabiners and rappel devices, his trusty tool kit, a beautifully-maintained Colt single action army revolver, and three neatly-folded military-style canvas sacks. He took off his hat and coat, and undressed rapidly.

Beneath the business suit he had worn for his visit to the bank was a specially-designed, close-fitting outfit with pockets for his tools of trade.

He stuffed the business clothes, day shoes, and hat inside the briefcase, stepped inside the moccasins, and tucked the gun in a rear pocket of the body suit. He shoved the floor plans inside his top before reaching into the left hand pocket of the coat. His fingers closed around a small, metal object. He took it out and smiled at the gold-colored key in his palm.

It was the one for the Yale lock on the bonds vault door. He had taken it from Thomson's suit pocket when the latter picked up his hat and swapped it for an almost identical key he had had made by a locksmith over a week ago. Since Howard was the last customer to use the vault late on a Friday afternoon, the forgery would not come to light until the following week, when Thomson next used the key.

Howard placed two of the canvas sacks into the third one and shrugged it onto his shoulders. Looping the rope around one arm, he took a lock pick from his tool kit and opened the rooftop door. An icy blast buffeted him when he stepped outside, the cold air driving his breath from his lungs. Sleet stung his face and pelted his thinly-clothed body.

The snowstorm had intensified in the hour that he had been inside the building; visibility across the rooftop was down to some ten feet. Howard closed the access door, tucked his head down, and marched briskly into the wind.

A large, rectangular-shaped structure loomed out of the gray landscape some fifty feet later. It was the roof of one of the elevator shafts. He stopped beside it, unscrewed a metal panel near the top, and dropped the briefcase and coat inside. He would retrieve them in a few hours.

He carried on toward the south end of the building and soon reached another metal structure. This one was smaller and circular in shape. It was one of the bank's six ventilation shafts.

Howard threaded the climbing rope through a rappel device which he secured around the base of a nearby metal pole, clipped the rope to the harness around his waist, and unscrewed the top of the shaft. He threw the ends of the rope down it and climbed inside. The noise of the storm abated almost immediately. A scattering of snowflakes danced down around him as he carefully dropped into the deepening gloom, the rope sliding smoothly between his gloved fingers.

He reached the base of the shaft some thirty feet later. Two branching ducts opened up at knee-level on either side of him. From his calculations, he was now on the tenth floor. He retrieved the rope, took a small torch from his tool kit, dropped to his knees, and crawled inside the left-hand passage.

It took another twenty minutes to reach the ventilation duct that ran across the ceiling of the anteroom on the seventh floor, where he had flirted with Thomson's secretary earlier that afternoon. Sweat beaded his face by the time he stopped next to a grille in the floor of the metal tube.

He switched his torch off and peered through the grating. Shadows filled the space beneath him. He made out the secretary's desk some ten feet below.

The bank's lights had been switched off. With winter upon the city and the snowstorm raging outside, little ambient light filtered through the building. He glanced at the luminous dials on his watch. It was nearly six o'clock.

Any minute now.

Right on cue, a beam of light cut through the gloom below him. The guards were making their first sweep of the bank, checking every office and corner of the building. According to the bank clerk he had interrogated, they would do another check at eight o'clock, before their shift change. Two more security sweeps would follow overnight, one at twelve and the second at four in the morning.

The clerk had also been quite generous with information concerning the alarm system in the bank's main vault. According to him, it was unparalleled in the Continental United States.

This had not unduly concerned Howard.

He watched the guard complete his rounds through the bonds offices before settling on his back inside the ventilation duct. All he had to do now was wait until eight o'clock to make his move. This would give him a window of a full four hours in which to get to the main vault before the guards made their midnight rounds.

The reason he had chosen not to hide somewhere more comfortable inside the building was that he had not wanted to risk running into any of the guards. Confrontation was not his strong point. Although he knew he could defend himself in most situations, blood made him squeamish. Besides, he had always prided himself on the fact he had committed one hundred percent of his burglaries without ever harming a single hair on anyone's head. His trademark was to get in and out of the building unseen.

The guard came around again two hours later, his movements rousing Howard from a light slumber. A chill raised goosebumps on his exposed skin as he carefully rolled over onto his front. The ambient temperature inside the ventilation system had dropped with nightfall.

He waited until the man's footsteps faded in the direction of the main hall before removing the screws from the corners of the grille. He moved the cover aside, gripped the edge of the opening, and carefully lowered himself down into the anteroom.

He landed on the secretary's desk with a soft thud. The motion jarred the candlestick telephone. It started to tilt over the edge of the table.

Howard jumped to the ground and caught the telephone a second before it struck the marble floor, his breath lodged somewhere in his throat. In the tomb-like silence of the building, the sound of the device falling would have carried all the way to the central corridor and the retreating guard's ears.

He blew out a sigh of relief and placed the telephone back on the table before heading silently down the passage on the left. He strolled past Thomson's office, stopped in front of the bonds vault, and removed the key he had stolen from the manager. He hesitated as he inserted it in the Yale lock.

This is where you find out whether you cocked things up or not.

He took a deep breath and twisted the key.

No alarms sounded. Howard thanked the blissful silence and pulled the steel door open.

A lingering acrid smell and a faint cloud of fumes greeted him inside the vault. He shone his torch on the door's interior and smiled at the melted mess of metal—all that was left of the compartment containing the time lock and alarm.

The device he had attached to the door earlier that afternoon was one of his specialities. Made of a series of tiny chambers inside a steel shell, it contained a timer and three glass vials of aqua regia, or nitro-hydrochloric acid. The corrosive mixture was capable of dissolving almost all metals, including gold and platinum. It had started to burn through the steel shell and the time lock panel exactly thirty minutes after Howard had engaged the switch designed to break the vials at a pre-set time.

Closing the vault door behind him, he retrieved the

stock certificates from the safety deposit box he had opened that afternoon and headed for the far wall.

He directed his torch beneath the table standing there. The light bounced off a metal grille in the floor.

It was an access point into the ventilation shaft that passed directly over the bank's main vault in the basement of the building. The only other access point large enough for a man to go through was in the bank's grand hall, where the guards were stationed.

When he examined the detailed floor plans of the building several weeks ago, Howard realized that to break into the bank's main vault by direct means would be a foolhardy endeavor. The best method of infiltrating and escaping the building unseen was to use a more roundabout route. That was when he noticed a possible way in through the ventilation system. Although the building's architects had designed the ducts in such a way that the one serving the basement vault tapered on its way toward the roof, making it impossible for anything smaller than a cat to get through from the top, let alone someone with his six-foot frame, they had to leave at least a few entry points large enough for service men to access the air system.

Howard unscrewed the metal grating and was inside the ventilation tunnel in less than a minute. Twenty feet later, he reached the first of several vertical drops. He took out the small trigger-switch, pistol-grip drill he had had made based on a new design by the Black & Decker power tool company, fixed a rappel device into the side wall, and dropped down the dark shaft.

His muscles shook slightly by the time he reached the basement nearly an hour later. Rappelling was not at the top of his list of favorite activities and he had had to do several practice sessions at the Devil's Lake Park outside Chicago to make sure he would not break a leg or his neck during the actual burglary.

Dying was not his main concern. He was more worried about being trapped inside the bank's ventilation system overnight. Enclosed spaces got to him after a while.

Excitement overcame fatigue when he gazed into the mouth of the tunnel that would take him to the ceiling of the main vault. He was less than an hour away from accomplishing the greatest heist of the decade. He climbed inside and started crawling.

The smell reached him when he was halfway to the vault. It got stronger the closer he drew to his target. Howard paused and wrinkled his nose.

There had better not be a dead rat up ahead.

He went around a corner a moment later and saw the final stretch to the finish line. He shone his light down the metal passage; the grille to the main vault was twenty feet from his current location.

An unpleasant jolt of adrenaline shot through Howard's veins when he glimpsed motion just beyond the reach of his torch beam.

'What the —?'

A large shape was moving along the tunnel from the other end of the shaft. It froze.

Howard's heart thundered inside his chest. *That's way too big to be a rat!*

He blinked when a bright light suddenly shone in his eyes. His alarm dissipated. Understanding bloomed in his mind. He scowled.

Oh no you don't, you bastard!

Howard gripped his torch in his mouth, whipped the revolver out of his back pocket, and crawled rapidly along the tunnel. A low grunt escaped the figure on the opposite side of the duct as it followed suit.

Howard reached the grille in the ceiling of the main vault at the same time as the other man. Steel-blue eyes glared at him from two feet away. The man was dressed in midnight-black clothes and wore a backpack.

'Who the hell are you?' hissed Howard. 'And what in *God's* name is that stench?'

'I could ask the same of you,' growled the stranger. He hesitated. 'I came in from the sewers.'

Howard narrowed his eyes. 'You'd have to go through several feet of steel-reinforced concrete. There's no access route to the ventilation system from the sewers.'

'There is now,' said the other man smugly.

Despite the clear danger of the situation he now found himself in, Howard could not help the flash of curiosity that darted through him. He lowered his torch.

'What'd you do? Use a pneumatic drill to break through the concrete?' He drew in a sharp breath, which he regretted almost immediately. 'Did you use explosives to blast your way through?'

'No, nothing that unrefined. I just used the power of my hands.'

Howard glanced down. He could make out some sort of star-shaped tattoo on the back of the man's left hand.

'Well buddy, I'm afraid the power of your hands is not going to stop me from being the one who robs this vault tonight. I was here first.'

He pointed his revolver at his rival.

An amused expression washed across the stranger's face. 'Oh, we're playing finders keepers?'

Howard nodded. 'Yep, so if you could be so kind as to remove yourself from this situation, I would really appreciate—'

He broke off at a sudden, metallic sound. The revolver shuddered in his hand. Howard looked down in time to see the rest of the pistol crumple into an unrecognizable lump. His jaw dropped.

The next thing he saw was a fist flying toward his face.

Pain exploded inside Howard's head as the stranger's knuckles connected with his nose. He felt something crunch.

'Unfortunately, I prefer to play losers weepers,' said the man with a hard smile.

Howard froze for a stunned second, uncertain which of the two lightning-fast events that had just unfolded he should be more shocked by. The agony of his physical injury won out.

'You *fuckthin basthard*, you broke my *nothe*!' he barked, gripping the affected appendage in question.

A warm trickle oozed into his palm. He looked down and grimaced at the drops of blood darkening his skin.

The other guy frowned. 'You were aiming a gun at my head.'

Howard stared at the remains of the revolver, anger and regret swirling in equal measure inside him.

'I won that off the Sundance Kid in a card game in 1891. I hadn't even loaded it.' He scowled. 'Do you know how valuable that gun was?'

The stranger studied him for a moment. 'Hmm.'

'What?' snapped Howard.

'Well, unless you were still being nursed at the time you played that card game, that can only mean one thing. You're an immortal.' The stranger made a face. 'And who brings an empty gun to a heist?'

'Someone who doesn't like to hurt people,' Howard retorted. He hesitated. 'So, you're an immortal too?'

'Uh-huh.'

Howard observed the stranger closely, his mind buzzing with dozens of questions.

Few humans in this world knew of the existence of the Crovirs and the Bastians, the two races of supernatural beings who walked among their kind and who were gifted with the ability to survive up to sixteen deaths. The immortals had been around for as long as mankind itself and had fought a bitter war that stretched across most of their history before its abrupt end in the fourteenth century, following a plague that wiped out more than half of the immortal population and made the overwhelming majority of survivors infertile.

These days, most immortals lived freely among humans, combining their duties to the Crovir and Bastian societies with their roles in the human world. But some chose to deny their affiliation with the immortal races and lived well outside their remit. Like his parents had.

'You a Bastian?' said Howard.

'No, Crovir. You?'

'Same here,' muttered Howard. 'How'd you find out about the gold?'

'From one of my informants in New York,' the stranger said with a shrug. 'You?'

'Heard two brokers talking about it a month ago.' Howard finally asked the question he had been dreading to voice. 'How'd you do it? How did you...crush the revolver to a pulp?'

The stranger glanced at the gun. 'I have certain... abilities.'

'Oh.' Howard brightened. 'You mean, like Houdini?'

The stranger grimaced. 'Don't compare me to that charlatan.'

'All right.' Howard touched his sore nose gingerly. 'What do I call you, Metal Boy?'

The other guy hesitated. 'My name is Storm. Ethan Storm.'

Howard paused before offering his hand. 'I'm Howard Titus.'

Even though Storm had broken his nose and wrecked his revolver, Howard could not help but admire the guy's style. Besides, it wasn't everyday he met another immortal thief. And one with seemingly magical powers at that.

Storm stared at his hand, nonplussed.

'You're supposed to shake it,' Howard said drily.

Storm reached out and shook his hand cautiously.

'You're a strange man, Titus,' he muttered gruffly.

Howard ignored the remark and looked at the grille. 'What should we do about this pickle we find ourselves in, Storm?'

Storm grunted. 'There's more than enough down there for the both of us, so I suggest you shut up and let me do my thing.'

Howard's mouth went dry as he watched the screws holding the metal grating undo themselves under the guy's influence. Storm pulled the loose cover, set it aside, and lowered himself through the opening. He dropped out of sight a second later.

Howard followed slowly and wondered whether he was making the biggest mistake of his thieving career. He landed in a low crouch next to his new companion, rose to his feet, and turned to shine his light at the dark space around them.

The vault was four times the size of the strongroom holding the bonds safety deposit boxes on the seventh floor. Although he had been aware of that fact from the floor plans, it still made for an impressive sight.

Giant metal cabinets bolted to the floor occupied one half of the room and looked upon a central corridor stretching to the massive steel door in the north wall of the vault. But the most spectacular thing of all was the sectioned-off space to the left, which took up the other half of the chamber.

Pallets and crates of gold and cash stood in orderly rows behind a thick wall of steel bars screwed into the ceiling and floor of the vault.

Howard's eyes glazed over slightly as he beheld the gleaming, yellow bars. 'Wow.'

Storm strolled to the door in the middle of the metal barrier and studied the lock. 'By the way, how exactly were you intending to get your loot out of here?'

Howard removed three steel devices similar to the one he had used to disable the time lock and alarm in the bonds vault from his pocket.

'These contain enough nitro-hydrochloric acid to melt through the security system on that door.' He indicated the vault opening. 'There's a service elevator at the other end of this basement. It goes to the goods entrance at the back of the building. It would be child's play to disable the alarm on it and gain access to the road.

My day clothes are in a briefcase at the bottom of the shaft.'

Storm turned and watched him with a curious expression. 'So, you were just going to walk out of here with bags of gold and cash?'

Howard grinned. 'Nope. I was going to put it at the bottom of one of the garbage bins outside the goods entrance. There's a collection truck that comes early tomorrow morning to take the rubbish to a landfill north of the city.'

Storm's lips curved in a small smile. 'That's clever.'

There was a clink from the lock. He pulled the steel door open.

Howard's pulse accelerated as he followed him inside the room. 'Can you manipulate things other than metal?'

Storm shrugged. 'Yes.'

Howard reeled at the enormity of what he was witnessing. Never had he heard of immortals possessing any other powers that those of fast healing, delayed aging, and the ability to survive all but their seventeenth death.

This is incredible. I could really use someone like him.

Cogs started to turn in his mind at that thought. He opened his mouth to voice the wondrous idea that had come to him.

'By the way, are you wearing tights?' said Storm.

Howard blinked, his trail of thought derailed by the guy's question. He looked down at his clothes.

'No. It's a specially made outfit.'

Storm's shoulders shook slightly as he turned to observe a pallet of gleaming gold bars. 'Oh.'

'Are you laughing at me?' Howard said coldly.

'No,' came the strangled reply.

Storm removed his backpack and took out another two bags from inside. He started to load cash and gold into the sacks.

Howard shrugged his canvas bag from his shoulders and filled his own sacks up with as much as he could carry. Fifteen minutes later, they were done loading up.

'How are *you* getting out of here?' Howard asked Storm.

'Me?' Storm smiled. 'I'm going back down into the sewers.'

Howard looked at the opening in the ceiling.

'What, through there?' he said dubiously.

'Yep. It's the safest route out of the building. There's no chance the guards will surprise me. Besides, that snowstorm's turned into a right blizzard.'

Howard made a face. 'But, it's the *sewers*.'

Storm shrugged. 'I've been in far worse places.'

Howard glanced at the vault door. He hesitated and wondered once more whether he was making a crazy decision.

'Mind if I tag along?'

Storm stilled at his words. He watched Howard for silent seconds, his expression unfathomable.

Howard could not help but feel that the immortal was erecting an invisible barrier between them.

Interesting. So this guy's a loner, like me.

Still, he sensed more than just a need for privacy in Storm's eyes. The immortal looked like he had retreated inside a thick shell that had taken decades to build.

'Sure,' Storm finally said.

They pushed one of the pallets under the hole in the ceiling and climbed on top. Storm went inside the ventilation shaft first and took the bags Howard passed up to him. He pulled him up after and screwed the metal grille back in place.

'Follow me,' Storm muttered. He led the way back in the direction he had come.

Howard moved after him.

With the bags in tow, it took them fifteen minutes to reach the opening Storm had made into the reinforced concrete separating the foundation of the building from the sewer system. Howard gazed beyond the rubble into the dark, festering pit where Storm was lowering his bags.

'You coming?' said the immortal quizzically, hands on the edges of the opening as he prepared to drop down into the hole.

Howard took a deep breath. *How bad can it be?*

HOWARD SLAMMED THE SHOT GLASS DOWN ON THE TABLE and wiped his mouth, a shudder running through him.

'Never again,' he murmured with heart-felt emotion.

The bathroom door opened. Storm strolled out and came down the passage, a towel around his shoulders. He was wearing the trousers Howard had lent him. They came up a couple of inches short at his ankles.

He stopped by the table. 'Are you still harping on about the sewers? You've led a really sheltered life, haven't you?'

Howard ignored him and sniffed at himself. 'Do I still smell? I feel like I reek. Maybe I need another shower.'

Storm rolled his eyes. 'You've already had two. That's why I ended up with cold water for mine.' He looked around the plainly-furnished apartment. 'I'm surprised. I thought your place would be more…flashy.'

With the blizzard having taken a firm hold on the city, Howard had invited Storm back to his place. It was not far from the business district and much closer than the motel where Storm was staying.

'This is only temporary lodging.'

He poured whisky into a second shot glass and pushed it toward Storm.

The immortal took it and sat at the table. He sipped the drink before indicating the bags on the floor. 'What are you going to do with the money?'

Howard leaned back in the chair and placed an ice pack on his nose. The swelling had already gone down, the injury healing at supernatural speed.

'Invest it, probably. Buy some land out west. You?'

Storm gazed into his glass. 'Build myself another life, in another city.'

He tilted his head and downed the whisky, his expression bleak.

Howard watched the immortal for a silent moment. He sensed a wealth of hidden meaning behind the man's bitter words.

This guy is really interesting.

He recalled the startling thought he'd had in the bank's vault.

'I think we should partner up,' he said abruptly.

Storm blinked at him. 'Huh?'

'With your abilities and my investment savvy, we could make several fortunes and live out the rest of our lives in luxury.'

Storm raised his eyebrows. 'Are you serious?'

Howard dipped his chin firmly. 'Yes.'

Storm frowned. 'I don't think so.'

'Oh come on, it'll be fun.' Howard gave him his most engaging smile. 'Besides, I've been looking for a business partner to team up with.'

No harm in a little white lie.

'I don't play well with others,' Storm said gruffly.

'You'll be won over by my charming personality.'

Storm opened and closed his mouth soundlessly, his expression uncertain.

Howard poured more whisky into the glasses. 'Tell you what, why don't you sleep on it?'

Storm took his drink with a guarded expression. 'I'm not going to change my mind.'

Howard hid a smile behind his glass. 'Sure, sure.'

He had sown the seed of doubt in Storm's mind. Now all he had to do was hound the guy into submission.

It was a challenge he was going to relish.

He clinked his glass against Storm's and raised it in the air. 'Here's to new friendships.'

Storm scowled.

THE END

Have you read Hunted, the first novel in AD's bestselling supernatural thriller series Seventeen featuring Lucas Soul? Turn the page to read an extract now!

HUNTED EXTRACT

PROLOGUE

My name is Lucas Soul.

Today, I died again.

This is my fifteenth death in the last four hundred and fifty years.

CHAPTER ONE

I woke up in a dark alley behind a building.

Autumn rain plummeted from an angry sky, washing the narrow, walled corridor I lay in with shades of gray. It dripped from the metal rungs of the fire escape above my head and slithered down dirty, barren walls, forming puddles under the garbage dumpsters by my feet. It gurgled in gutters and rushed in storm drains off the main avenue behind me.

It also cleansed away the blood beneath my body.

For once, I was grateful for the downpour; I did not want any evidence left of my recent demise.

I blinked at the drops that struck my face and slowly climbed to my feet. Unbidden, my fingers rose to trace the cut in my chest; the blade had missed the birthmark on my skin by less than an inch.

I turned and studied the tower behind me. I was not sure what I was expecting to see. A face peering over the edge of the glass and brick structure. An avenging figure drifting down in the rainfall, a bloodied sword in its hands and a crazy smile in its eyes. A flock of silent crows come to take my unearthly body to its final resting place.

Bar the heavenly deluge, the skyline was fortunately empty.

I pulled my cell phone out of my jeans and stared at it. It was smashed to pieces. I sighed. I could hardly blame the makers of the device. They had probably never tested it from the rooftop of a twelve-storey building. As for me, the bruises would start to fade by tomorrow.

It would take another day for the wound in my chest to heal completely.

I glanced at the sky again before walking out of the alley. An empty phone booth stood at the intersection to my right. I strolled toward it and closed the rickety door behind me. A shiver wracked my body while I dialed a number. Steam soon fogged up the glass wall before me.

There was a soft click after the fifth ring.

'Yo,' said a tired voice.

'Yo yourself,' I said.

A yawn traveled down the line. 'What's up?'

'I need a ride. And a new phone.'

There was a short silence. 'It's four o'clock in the morning.' The voice had gone blank.

'I know,' I said in the same tone.

The sigh at the other end was audible above the pounding of the rain on the metal roof of the booth. 'Where are you?'

'Corner of Cambridge and Staniford.'

Fifteen minutes later, a battered, tan Chevrolet Monte Carlo pulled up next to the phone box. The passenger door opened.

'Get in,' said the figure behind the wheel.

I crossed the sidewalk and climbed in the seat. Water dripped onto the leather cover and formed a puddle by my feet. There was a disgruntled mutter from my left. I looked at the man beside me.

Reid Hasley was my business partner and friend. Together, we co-owned the Hasley and Soul Agency. We were private investigators, of sorts. Reid certainly qualified as one, being a former Marine and cop. I, on the other hand, had been neither.

'You look like hell,' said Reid as he maneuvered the car into almost nonexistent traffic. He took something from his raincoat and tossed it across to me. It was a new cell.

I raised my eyebrows. 'That was fast.'

He grunted indistinct words and lit a cigarette. 'What happened?' An orange glow flared into life as he inhaled, casting shadows under his brow and across his nose.

I transferred the data card from the broken phone into the new one and frowned at the bands of smoke drifting toward me. 'That's going to kill you one day.'

'Just answer the question,' he retorted.

I looked away from his intense gaze and contemplated

the dark tower at the end of the avenue. 'I met up with our new client.'

'And?' said Reid.

'He wasn't happy to see me.'

Something in my voice made him stiffen. 'How unhappy are we talking here?'

I sighed. 'Well, he stuck a sword through my heart and pushed me off the top of the Cramer building. I'd say he was pretty pissed.'

Silence followed my words. 'That's not good,' said Reid finally.

'No.'

'It means we're not gonna get the money,' he added.

'I'm fine by the way. Thanks for asking,' I said.

He shot a hard glance at me. 'We need the cash.'

Unpalatable as the statement was, it was also regrettably true. Small PI firms like ours had just about managed before the recession. Nowadays, people had more to worry about than what their cheating spouses were up to. Although embezzlement cases were up by a third, the victims of such scams were usually too hard up to afford the services of a good detective agency. As a result, the rent on our office space was overdue by a month.

Mrs. Trelawney, our landlady, was not pleased about this; at five-foot two and weighing just over two hundred pounds, the woman had the ability to make us quake in our boots. This had less to do with her size than the fact that she made the best angel cakes in the city. She gave them out to her tenants when they paid the rent on time. A month without angel cakes was making us twitchy.

'I think we might still get the cakes if you flash your eyes at her,' mused my partner.

I stared at him. 'Are you pimping me out?'

'No. You'd be a tough sell,' he retorted as the car splashed along the empty streets of the city. He glanced at me. 'This makes it what, your fourteenth death?'

'Fifteenth.'

His eyebrows rose. 'Huh. So, two more to go.'

I nodded mutely. In many ways, I was glad Hasley had entered my unnatural life, despite the fact that it happened in such a dramatic fashion. It was ten years ago this summer.

Hasley was a detective in the Boston PD Homicide Unit at the time. One hot Friday afternoon in August, he and his partner of three years found themselves on the trail of a murder suspect, a Latino man by the name of Burt Suarez. Suarez worked the toll bridge northeast of the city and had no priors. Described by his neighbors and friends as a gentle giant who cherished his wife, was kind to children and animals, and even attended Sunday service, the guy did not have so much as a speeding ticket to his name. That day, the giant snapped and went on a killing spree after walking in on his wife and his brother in the marital bed. He shot Hasley's partner, two uniformed cops, and the neighbor's dog, before fleeing toward the river.

Unfortunately, I got in his way.

In my defense, I had not been myself for most of that month, having recently lost someone who had been a friend for more than a hundred years. In short, I was drunk.

On that scorching summer's day, Burt Suarez achieved

something no other human, or non-human for that matter, had managed before or since.

He shot me in the head.

Sadly, he did not get to savor this feat, as he died minutes after he fired a round through my skull. Hasley still swore to this day that Suarez's death had more to do with seeing me rise to my feet Lazarus-like again than the gunshot wound he himself inflicted on the man with his Glock 19.

That had been my fourteenth death. Shortly after witnessing my unholy resurrection, Hasley quit his job as a detective and became my business partner.

Over the decade that followed, we trailed unfaithful spouses, found missing persons, performed employee checks for high profile investment banks, took on surveillance work for attorneys and insurance companies, served process to disgruntled defendants, and even rescued the odd kidnapped pet. Hasley knew more about me than anyone else in the city.

He still carried the Glock.

'Why did he kill you?' said Reid presently. He braked at a set of red lights. 'Did you do something to piss him off?' There was a trace of suspicion in his tone. The lights turned green.

'Well, broadly speaking, he seemed opposed to my existence.' The rhythmic swishing of the windscreen wipers and the dull hiss of rubber rolling across wet asphalt were the only sounds that broke the ensuing lull. 'He called me an ancient abomination that should be sent straight to Hell and beyond.' I grimaced. 'Frankly, I thought that was a bit ironic coming from someone who's probably not that much older than me.'

Reid crushed the cigarette butt in the ashtray and narrowed his eyes. 'You mean, he's one of you?'

I hesitated before nodding once. 'Yes.'

Over the years, as I came to know and trust him, I told Reid a little bit about my origins.

I was born in Europe in the middle of the sixteenth century, when the Renaissance was at its peak. My father came from a line of beings known as the Crovirs, while my mother was a descendant of a group called the Bastians. They are the only races of immortals on Earth.

Throughout most of the history of man, the Crovirs and the Bastians have waged a bitter and brutal war against one another. Although enough blood has been shed over the millennia to fill a respectable portion of the Caspian Sea, this unholy battle between immortals has, for the most, remained a well-kept secret from the eyes of ordinary humans, despite the fact that they have been used as pawns in some of its most epic chapters.

The conflict suffered a severe and unprecedented setback in the fourteenth century, when the numbers of both races dwindled rapidly and dramatically; while the Black Death scourged Europe and Asia, killing millions of humans, the lesser-known Red Death shortened the lives of countless immortals. It was several decades before the full extent of the devastation was realized, for the plague had brought with it an unexpected and horrifying complication.

The greater part of those who survived became infertile.

This struck another blow to both sides and, henceforth, an uneasy truce was established. Although the odd incident still happened between embittered members of each race, the fragile peace has, surprisingly, lasted to this day. From that time on, the arrival of an immortal child into the world became an event that was celebrated at the highest levels of each society.

My birth was a notable exception. The union between a Crovir and a Bastian was considered an unforgivable sin and strictly forbidden by both races; ancient and immutable, it was a fact enshrined into the very doctrines and origins of our species. Any offspring of such a coupling was thus deemed an abomination unto all and sentenced to death from the very moment they were conceived. I was not the first half-breed, both races having secretly mated with each other in the past. However, the two immortal societies wanted me to be the last. Fearing for my existence, my parents fled and took me into hiding.

For a while, our life was good. We were far from rich and dwelled in a remote cabin deep in the forest, where we lived off the land, hunting, fishing, and even growing our own food. Twice a year, my father ventured down the mountain to the nearest village, where he traded fur for oil and other rare goods. We were happy and I never wanted for anything.

It was another decade before the Hunters finally tracked us down. That was when I learned one of the most important lessons about immortals.

We can only survive up to sixteen deaths.

Having perished seven times before, my father died after ten deaths at the hands of the Hunters. He fought until the very last breath left his body. I watched them kill my mother seventeen times.

I should have died that day. I did, in fact, suffer my

very first death. Moments after the act, I awoke on the snow-covered ground, tears cooling on my face and my blood staining the whiteness around me. Fingers clenching convulsively around the wooden practice sword my father had given me, I waited helplessly for a blade to sink into my heart once more. Minutes passed before I realized I was alone in that crimson-colored clearing, high up in the Carpathian Mountains.

The crows came next, silent flocks that descended from the gray winter skies and covered the bloodied bodies next to me. When the birds left, the remains of my parents had disappeared as well. All that was left was ash.

It was much later that another immortal imparted to me the theory behind the seventeen deaths. Each one apparently took away a piece of our soul. Unlike our bodies, our souls could not regenerate after a death. Thus, Death as an ultimate end was unavoidable. And then the crows come for most of us.

No one was really clear as to where the birds took our earthly remains.

'What if you lived alone, on a desert island or something, and never met anyone? You could presumably never die,' Reid had argued with his customary logic when I told him this.

'True. However, death by boredom is greatly underestimated,' I replied. 'Besides, someone like you is bound to kill himself after a day without a smoke.'

'So the meeting was a trap?' said Reid.

His voice jolted me back to the present. The car had pulled up in front of my apartment block. The road ahead was deserted.

'Yes.' Rain drummed the roof of the Monte Carlo. The

sound reminded me of the ricochets of machine guns. Unpleasant memories rose to the surface of my mind. I suppressed them firmly.

'Will he try to kill you again?' said Reid. I remained silent. He stared at me. 'What are you gonna do?'

I shifted on the leather seat and reached for the door handle. 'Well, seeing as you're likely to drag me back from Hell if I leave you high and dry, I should probably kill him first.'

I exited the car, crossed the sidewalk, and entered the lobby of the building. I turned to watch the taillights of the Chevrolet disappear in the downpour before getting in the lift. Under normal circumstances, I would have taken the stairs to the tenth floor. Dying, I felt, was a justifiable reason to take things easy for the rest of the night.

My apartment was blessedly cool and devoid of immortals hell-bent on carving another hole in my heart. I took a shower, dressed the wound on my chest, and went to bed.

Get Hunted now!

ACKNOWLEDGMENTS

To all my friends who helped make this possible. You know who you are.

To you, my readers. Thank you for reading The Seventeen Series Ultimate Short Story Collection. If you enjoyed my book, please consider leaving a review on Goodreads or on the store where you purchased it. Reviews help readers like you find my books and I truly appreciate your honest opinions about my stories.

Make sure to sign up to my store newsletter for special deals on my books and new release alerts. Or you can sign up to my author newsletter to get upcoming release notifications, sneak peeks, and giveaways.

BOOKS BY A.D. STARRLING

SEVENTEEN NOVELS

Hunted

Warrior

Empire

Legacy

Origins

Destiny

SEVENTEEN SHORT STORIES

First Death

Dancing Blades

The Meeting

The Warrior Monk

The Hunger

The Bank Job

The Seventeen Series Ultimate Short Story Collection (#1-6)

LEGION

Blood and Bones

Fire and Earth

Awakening

Forsaken

Hallowed Ground

Heir

Legion

ABOUT A.D. STARRLING

Visit Shop AD Starrling and buy all of AD's ebooks, paperbacks, hardbacks, audiobooks, and exclusive special edition print books direct.

Want to know about AD Starrling's upcoming releases? Sign up to her author newsletter for new release alerts, sneak peeks, giveaways, and more.

Follow AD Starrling on Amazon.

Join AD's reader group on Facebook
The Seventeen Club.

Check out this link to find out more about A.D. Starrling
Linktr.ee/AD_Starrling.

www.ingramcontent.com/pod-product-compliance
Lightning Source LLC
Chambersburg PA
CBHW031246120726

47905CB00002B/743